# SOMETHING TO BELIEVE IN

Whiskey Mountain Book 3

Samantha Baca

**Whiskey Mountain**

## Whiskey Mountain Series

Something To Talk About
Something To Think About
Something To Believe In
Something To Live For

Content Warning

This book contains language and storylines that may be bothersome for some readers and is intended for a mature audience. Sexual scenes may be shown in detail as well. The reader is encouraged to reach out to the author directly (authorsamanthabaca@gmail.com) if they would like to further discuss the content warning(s) for this book.

Please note the following items that come up briefly in the book:

Dementia (secondary character)

# Contents

# One

## Dylan

My palms were sweaty as I waited in line, staring at the chalkboard menu hanging on the wall. I had been to Cravings once since it opened, but it was for their grand opening, and I didn't have to order anything because there were samples out for everyone to try.

Now that I was here as a paying customer, there was a lot of pressure to place a simple order without embarrassing myself in front of Calli, the owner. It wasn't that I was stupid and didn't know how to; it was that she was the hottest woman I had ever laid eyes on, and that made me a nervous wreck.

The line moved in front of me, putting me closer to being in the spotlight. I swallowed hard, pulling at the neck of my t-shirt that suddenly felt like it was choking me. It was hot outside, but the temperature rose to unbearable heights the moment her eyes caught mine. I was burning up and sweaty—two very unattractive qualities to showcase right now.

I tried not to stare as she stood behind the counter, tucking a loose strand of curly blonde hair behind her ear while she took the older man's order. She was so patient—and possibly oblivious—as he made passes at her, shamelessly flirting as his wife smacked his arm with her handbag.

It was hard not to laugh as the older couple trotted off, the woman still hitting him as he did his best to convince her he wasn't hitting on Calli. I'd known the Thompsons since I was a little boy, and the whole town knew how big of a flirt George was.

"Are you ready?" she asked, startling me as her blue eyes lit up.

I looked around to find that everyone in front of me had moved on and was either filling their cups or waiting for their food.

"Oh, yeah," I stammered, forcing my feet to move forward without face-planting in front of her. "Sorry, I wasn't paying attention."

"It's not a problem," she said sweetly, with a warm grin. "What can I get you?"

"I'll have you."

Her brows rose slightly in surprise, her lips pressed together as she tried to keep from laughing.

At least she found it humorous, while all I wanted to do was smack myself upside the head. *Why did I say that?*

"I'm sorry," I apologized, clearing my throat. "I'll have you."

She lifted her hand and covered her smile behind it, bubble gum pink nails catching my eye.

I took a deep breath and slowly released it, not trusting myself to speak to her. This was going even worse than I had imagined. I could talk to people all day, every day, but give me a beautiful woman I felt attracted to, and I was a bumbling mess.

"I don't know what's wrong with me," I muttered, shaking my head and lowering it. I was ready to turn around and get the hell out of there, vowing never to return.

"You probably have low blood sugar," Ramona said, sneaking up on me and putting her arm around my shoulders. Leave it to my best friend to swoop in and save the day. "It's late in the day, and you probably skipped breakfast if I know you."

I turned my head and looked at her, relief washing over me that she was there so I wouldn't keep embarrassing myself.

"I hate getting low blood sugar," Calli replied. "It's the worst, and I feel like I'm in this fog until they come back up."

"Right? It's such a pain. I can usually cure mine with a bag of Cool Ranch Doritos." Ramona laughed, but I knew how serious she was about her chips. It was nice of her to save me from myself, even if it was something as silly as low blood sugar—which I didn't get, but she did often. Way too often.

"Well, I only have a few minutes before I need to get back to Cool Cats. What do you recommend today, Calli?" Ramona gave my shoulder a quick squeeze before releasing me.

"The spicy tuna wrap is always good for hot days, but if you don't want fish, I would go with the chicken and waffles."

"Oooh, spicy tuna sounds delicious. Let me get two of those, please," Ramona said, looking at me. "Do you want one too? They have a club sandwich on the board as well, if you'd rather that."

I loved how well she knew me and that she could tell I was still freezing up around Calli.

"The club would be perfect. Thank you." I cleared my throat again and then forced myself to stop before Calli started to think I was sick or something.

"Is it together or separate?" Calli asked, her fingers hovering above the register keys.

"Together." Ramona smiled and slid her card across the counter.

"No, I've got it," I objected before Ramona's hand darted out and slapped mine as I tried to pull her card back.

Calli raised her eyebrows and studied us, waiting before trying to take the card.

"I've got it," Ramona confirmed through somewhat gritted teeth.

I narrowed my eyes at her, knowing she knew how much I hated it when she did that.

"You didn't need to buy me lunch," I said as soon as we walked away to fill our cups.

"I know. It's my treat."

"Well, thank you. I appreciate it. You know how I feel about you paying for stuff for me, though."

"Oh, whatever." She waved her hand dismissively as she filled her cup with root beer. "If you really wanted to repay me, you could grab a carton of vanilla ice cream and bring it over to Cool Cats so we can make floats. That would be heavenly. It's too freaking hot out for the middle of August."

"As much as I would love to, I have to get back to work. Raincheck?"

"Of course."

We waited to the side while they made our order. Ramona was making small talk, telling me something about Preston and their progress with training their dog, Rosco, but I couldn't focus because I couldn't take my eyes off Calli.

She had the most perfect smile that brightened her eyes and lit up her face. Everyone around her seemed happier, too. It was like she could change anyone's mood just by smiling.

I felt eyes on me and looked down to find Ramona watching me with a shit-eating grin spread across her cheeks. Apparently, even I was smiling just watching her.

"What?" I asked when she continued to stare without saying anything.

"Nothing." She shrugged.

"Liar."

A young, scrawny kid grabbed a tray and loaded our order, sitting it on the counter before calling Ramona's name.

"I was just thinking about how you've got it bad. So freaking bad." She laughed and walked off, leaving me standing there feeling like a complete love-sick teenager.

# Two
## Calli

"I cannot believe how busy we've been," Paisley said, sitting down across from me at the table.

The rush finally died shortly after Dylan and Ramona left, leaving us with a slow trickle until we closed at 3:30.

"I know, it's incredible. I wasn't sure what to expect when I first signed the lease on this building, but I can say it's going better than I ever imagined."

"I told you, have faith, and good things will come."

I smiled at my best friend, thankful she had followed me and my heart to Whiskey Mountain, Montana. Technically, we were right smack on the line between Whiskey Mountain and Fallen Oaks, two very small towns that were growing by the minute.

"I'm trying," I sighed heavily, leaning back against the chair. "It's a lot all at once."

"I know. But I'm here to help. Lean on me and we'll figure all of this out together."

I nodded, too tired to say anything more.

I'd had no plans to leave Miami before my mom was diagnosed with dementia and needed my help. I packed up everything and moved to Whiskey Mountain, bringing Paisley along with me with no clue what I was going to do until I got here.

It wasn't that I didn't want to be here; it was just that I had no idea what I was going to do. I was used to big city life, and going to a small town where I knew no one made it hard to take that initial jump and trust that I could handle starting over.

I had worked at an upscale restaurant in Miami, but it was nothing compared to owning and running my own—something I had always dreamed of. When I first got to Whiskey Mountain, I stopped to get coffee at this cute little shop called Spill The Beans. It was there that I learned that they were looking to develop the area that was currently deserted aside from a cute little pet shop. Lo-and-behold, there just so happened to be a vacant spot left, which was perfect for a restaurant.

I cashed in my 401K, made a wish on a star, and never looked back.

"Your mom seems to enjoy it," Paisley noted, glancing at my mom sitting at a table in the corner, people-watching.

"I think so, too. Her doctor said it was good for her to be as involved as she wanted. It makes me more comfortable having her here with me than worrying about her being alone at home. I'm hoping that if she's here every day—or most days of the week when I'm here — that it'll be familiar to her. Plus, she enjoys helping with the menu."

"It was a genius idea." Paisley laughed. "Changing the menu every day depending on her cravings has been fun for the locals. There's nothing else like it around here."

"She always loved cooking, and if I can keep part of that alive for her, I'm going to. Once I get someone hired to take over up front, I can get back to the kitchen and have her help me. I think she'll really love that."

I smiled and watched as she sipped her afternoon tea, a look of peace and tranquility etched on her face.

# Three
## Dylan

I wiped the sweat from my brow and climbed down the ladder, ready to be done for the day. The sun was hotter than the devil's playground, making my mounting headache worse. Add on the overwhelming smell of tar, and it was a recipe for a migraine.

The job went later today than it should have, but we had a new guy who didn't know shit about roofing, which was what had kept us going longer than usual. I opened the top of the giant jug of water and began chugging, tempted to dump the other half over my head to cool me off.

"Good work up there today," Curtis said, nodding up to where the rest of the guys were collecting their supplies and coming down.

"Thanks. Should have been finished hours ago."

"I know. He'll learn. Everyone has to start somewhere."

"Well, maybe have them start elsewhere during the summer months so the rest of us don't have to suffer," I joked, giving him a wink so he knew I was playing.

"Hell no. This is the ultimate test to see if they have what it takes. See what they're made of."

"I hate to break it to you, but he's not cut out for this." I jerked my head to the side where the new guy was bent over the gravel, heaving.

"Fuck," Curtis said, rubbing a hand down his face in frustration. "We have six more jobs to get done before the end of September. I needed him to work out."

He heaved louder, drawing the attention of a few of the guys. No one went over to check on him, having seen this a handful of times already. Some guys could handle the physical labor of roofing and others couldn't. It was always easy to spot those ones.

"I'll start on the other building tomorrow," I offered, pulling another drink in. "I can be there by 4. Have Soliz and Lowry meet me there and send the other guys to finish this one. We can crank these out quicker if we work early in the morning before it gets too hot."

"Thanks, Dylan. You're gonna have a ton of overtime this week."

I knew he couldn't afford to keep paying me the overtime I was accruing, and given that he was my dad's best friend, I also couldn't take advantage of it either.

"How about we forget about the overtime, and you give me two weeks off once this project is done?"

"If you can crank out the last six retail shops before our deadline, I'll give you a full month off."

I arched my eyebrow, always enjoying a good bet.

"Yeah?"

"Yup. But I can't give you any more help than what you already have."

"And I can work whatever hours I need to?"

"Whatever it takes to get the job done *right*."

"Ha," I scoffed. "Have I ever *not* done a job right? I'm the image of perfection, don't you remember?"

I felt the dimples in my cheeks deepen with my grin.

Curtis rolled his eyes and pretended he wasn't amused.

"Yeah, and you get your humbled charm from your dad."

We both laughed, then he went off to talk to the new guy while I collected my stuff and got the hell out of there. Tomorrow was going to be a long day, which meant that I needed to shower and hit the sack early tonight.

*************

Morning came quicker than I would have liked, given that I slept like shit and could use a few more hours of sleep. Wanting to keep my end of the bargain up for Curtis meant I needed to get over it and get my ass to the job site.

I loved that there were no cars on the road, no one to get in my way as I started the day. The only downside was that most of the businesses in Whiskey Mountain didn't open until 9, which meant that I was stuck with a crappy cup of coffee from home for my caffeine fix. I could have grabbed some energy drinks after I left last night, but I was exhausted and just wanted to go home. Today, I regretted that decision tenfold.

It was amazing to see how much had been developed in the small stretch between Whiskey Mountain and Fallen Oaks in just the past year. After a dangerous blizzard stranded Ramona with no easy access to necessities, her fiancé rallied everyone together and got the ball rolling on developing this part of town.

Since then, several other shops had opened around her pet store, and business was booming. Cravings was still the only restaurant, but there were plans to bring in a coffee shop and an upscale steakhouse as soon as the construction was completed.

The portion that we were working on was right next to Cravings and would be a smaller strip mall on Main Street, plus the movie theater that was right beside it, at the end of the street. The town locals were excited about that, given that the closest movie theater was over an hour away.

I grabbed my supplies and carried them up with me, heading down for another load when Soliz and Lowry showed up. I had worked with them for so long that we gave each other a quick nod as a greeting, and all got to work. I grabbed my tool belt and was securing it around my waist when I saw the door to Cravings open.

"Hey, I thought I heard someone out here," Calli said, peeking around the door. It was still dark out, only a few streetlights illuminating her features.

"Sorry if we bothered you. I didn't think anyone would be here this early."

"Nope, you didn't. I'm used to being aware of my surroundings and investigating every noise I hear after living in a big city." She laughed, pushing the door open and resting her shoulder against it as her arms folded across her chest. "So, what are you doing here so early?"

I nodded to the roof where the other guys were and then looked at her.

"We're working on the roofs on this side of the strip mall. I was hoping we'd get here before anyone opened so we could crank out the loud parts and not disrupt business."

She leaned forward and looked up before looking back at me.

"I didn't know you were a roofer."

"One of the best," I said with a cheesy grin and a wink. My palms started to sweat, and I suddenly felt all twitchy again.

"Well, I won't keep you so you can get started. I'll be here if you need water or coffee or anything. Just come on in."

"Thank you, I appreciate that. Why are you here so early?"

She yawned and tried to hide it behind her hand.

"My mom wanted biscuits and gravy this morning, so I came in early to get a head start on the food prep for the day. Everything she's talked about since last night has been a combination of breakfast foods, so that's what today's menu will be focused on. I'm going to be making some pastries, too. Stop by and try one if you'd like. I'll be sure to make those lemon blueberry donuts you like so much."

My cheeks flushed as she chewed her lower lip. She was right—I fucking loved those donuts. She had made them for the grand opening at Cool Cats when Ramona expanded and added a pet daycare, but I didn't expect her to notice.

"I'll be sure to come by to grab one in a bit. I brought coffee from home—"

She scrunched her nose in the most adorable way.

"What?" I asked playfully, a laugh floating off of my lips. "What's that face for?"

"What kind of coffee did you make?"

"I don't know. Black? It was that instant coffee you get in the can and add it to hot water."

"Noooo," she cried out, her face twisted in disgust. "That's not real coffee!"

"You sound just like my friend, Maggie. She takes coffee pretty seriously, too."

"Maggie from Spill The Beans?"

I nodded, feeling guilty for leaving the guys to work without me while I talked to Calli. But nothing could have torn me away from her now that I had her alone and could finally get actual words out of my mouth.

"The one and only," I confirmed.

"Well, Maggie is right. That's not real coffee. Now I can't make the incredible lattes that she makes, but I can make you a decent cup of coffee. Do you have a few minutes to come inside?"

I looked up at the roof, wondering how much the guys were going to hate me.

"I'll send you with coffee for them too. You'll be their new favorite once they taste my cold brew."

"Yeah, sure. I've got a few minutes," I said, forcing my feet to move and my heart to stop racing.

# Four
## Calli

"So, what do you think?" I pressed my fingers together in front of me and watched as Dylan took a sip.

His dark hair was buzzed and begged for me to run my hands over it. I imagined it was to keep him cool while working in the summer heat, but it also just looked incredible on him. Not that I was checking him out or anything.

"That's delicious," he said, setting his glass down and swiping his tongue over his upper lip to catch the tiny drops of the vanilla sweet cream cold foam. "That might be the best iced coffee I've ever had—don't tell Maggie I said that."

I giggled and shook my head.

"It will be our secret."

I couldn't help but look away as a rush of heat brushed across my cheeks. There were plenty of things I wanted to be *our secret*. But now wasn't the time to think those kinds of thoughts about him.

"Do you want 2 more to go for your friends?" I asked, grabbing the pitcher from the counter.

"Sure, that would be great. Thank you."

I smiled and prepared their drinks, thankful I had a few moments alone with Dylan without the rush of customers keeping me distracted.

I lined up the drinks, wiped them down after adding the

foam, and then set them in a drink tray to make it easier for him to get them up there.

"How much do I owe you?" he asked, reaching for his wallet.

"Nothing." I held my hands up to stop him. "There's no charge."

He pulled his head back and frowned, wallet in hand, ready to pay.

"I'm not taking these for free. Please tell me how much they are."

I tugged my lip between my teeth, trying to force some of the nervous energy out of me. Only it wasn't just nervous energy but more of an excited energy, and I worried that if I didn't do something to keep myself busy, I would jump over the counter and kiss him.

"They're free." I shrugged.

"No, they're not. Please let me pay."

"I can't do that."

"And why not?"

"Because I don't sell cold brew. I sell basic coffee, like the kind you can make at home." I scrunched my face the same way I had when he told me what he had made.

"You don't sell this?"

I shook my head.

"Then why did you make it for me?"

"I couldn't stand the thought of you drinking that crap from home." I laughed, covering my mouth before I accidentally snorted.

"The same crap you serve to customers here?" he teased, his voice going sexily lower.

I nodded.

"Well, thank you for the drink. You didn't have to make one for the guys, too. I feel bad now that you won't let me pay you."

"It wasn't a problem at all. Plus, I knew you would need something to bribe them with since you took forever to get up there. I didn't want you to get picked on." I winked playfully.

"Eh, I've been around those guys so long that they know better. But seriously, thanks again. And if you ever need help with anything or have any roof-related issues—just let me know."

"I think I'm good there," I laughed. "Now, if you said you could fix a leaky pipe, that would be a different story."

I expected him to laugh and say something like—*yeah, no can do*. Instead, he gave me a smirk that made my insides melt.

"I'll be done around 4 today. If you need me before then, just let me know. Otherwise, I'll be back around then."

He winked and carried the drink tray tucked into his side before letting the door close behind him. I sagged against the counter, feeling the tingles spread through me and light my body on fire.

# Five

## Dylan

I'd never been more excited to work on a leaky pipe than I was to fix Calli's. The day dragged on, my excitement to see her overriding everything else. Being around Calli was like going to Disneyland and having no lines to wait in. Not that I was comparing her to a ride—though I also wouldn't mind riding her either.

I shook my head to clear the dirty thoughts as I packed up the last of my tools and carried them down to my truck. I gave a quick wave to the guys as they took off, then gave myself a pep-talk before heading inside.

Cravings was already empty, having closed a few minutes ago. I smiled at the employees who were cleaning up and scanned the room, looking for Calli. I didn't want anyone to think I was *that guy* who came in after they were closed and still expected to be served. I knew a few of the young kids who worked there, but the rest were all new faces.

"Can I help you?"

I spun around, startled by the girl behind me. She was young, around Calli's age, if I had to guess, with emerald green eyes and jet-black hair that made them look even more fierce.

"Hi, um, I'm looking for Calli." I cleared my throat, hating that it had taken over as a new nervous tick every time I said her name.

"She's in the office, back by the kitchen. You can go on back." She nodded, then gave me a smile that made me curious to know what Calli might have said to her about me.

I smacked my lips together, trying to play it cool but looking like a doofus instead. I refrained from showing my embarrassment as I headed through the double doors into the kitchen. There was a radio playing music from the back of the room, and if I stopped moving, I could hear the faint sound of someone singing.

Not just anyone, Calli. And she wasn't just singing. She was singing a note so beautiful that even the angels in heaven would weep over it.

I made my way toward the office, not wanting to interrupt her. I could listen to her sing all day, every day. Hell, I would be ecstatic to sit down and record her singing just so I could use it as my daily playlist while working. It would make work a lot more pleasant, and the days would fly by just hearing the beautiful tone of her voice.

I paused by the door, waiting a few seconds before knocking as I listened to her sing along with Adele. Goosebumps spread across my skin quicker than lightning, my heart beating wildly in my chest as I soaked in every word that came out of her mouth.

"She's a good singer, isn't she?"

My head whipped around, startled again. I leaned forward a bit to read her name tag so at least I would know who the heck it was that kept sneaking up on me.

"Wonderful," I said quietly, hoping Calli couldn't hear us.

"I always told her she belonged on stage with her own music label, but she never believed me." Paisley stood next to me, smiling so big that it stretched across her cheeks.

"Have you known each other long?" I asked, keeping my voice low.

"Since we were babies. We grew up together."

"Wow. That's pretty awesome."

"Yeah, she's more like a sister to me than anything. I lost my mom when I was little, so her mom has always been like a second mom to me. She took me in and raised me right alongside Calli. Never complained about it a day in her life."

I smiled softly, eager to hear more about Calli's life.

"But you can't stand out here all day," Paisley said, shaking her head. "If you want to get that girl, you're gonna have to try harder."

"I—" I snapped my mouth shut. "That's not what I'm here for."

She raised an eyebrow while her mouth pulled to the side in a mischievous grin.

"No?"

I shook my head, trying to force the logical thoughts loose so they would float down and come out of my mouth.

"Calli asked me to fix her pipes. She's leaking."

Paisley's eyebrows shot higher on her forehead as her lips pressed into a thin line to keep from laughing.

*Fuck. Why did I say that?*

My mind was constantly mush whenever Calli was involved. I cleared my throat again and started over.

"I apologize. I meant to say that *they're* leaking. She has a leak somewhere, and I'm here to fix her. It. *Fix it.*" I swallowed hard, my throat uncomfortably dry.

I suddenly wished that the earth would just open and swallow me.

"I thought I heard voices," Calli said, peeking around the door. "Did I hear you say that I'm leaking?"

She gave me a cheeky grin, grabbed her water bottle from

behind her, and came out.

"I say a lot of stupid shit lately," I mumbled, running a hand through my hair, remembering that I needed to shave my head again soon.

"Eh, we all do. Don't worry about it. How about we deal with the pipes in the bathroom for now, and we can worry about whatever leaks I have later?"

Calli tossed a wink over her shoulder as she led the way, but I couldn't help but pick up the flirty undertone in her words.

"You two have fun," Paisley called.

The hall was brightly lit with sconces adorning the walls next to framed family pictures. I wanted to stop and look but didn't want to be rude to Calli since she had asked for help with plumbing. I turned my head forward to focus but caught a glimpse of a photo that made me stop in my tracks.

I grinned as I looked at a faded portrait in an antique-looking frame of a toddler girl wearing a chef hat and apron, her face painted red with spaghetti sauce as she proudly held handfuls of noodles in each hand. Her grin was contagious, and I felt a tug at my heart as I realized it was Calli.

She stood next to me, smiling at the photo, but I could feel some tension coming from her.

"I was three," she said softly. "I told my mom I wanted to be a chef, so she got me the outfit. I wore it proudly every time I cooked. My dad was such a trickster and loved playing practical jokes. It was his idea to grab the giant balls of spaghetti to see how much I could hold at one time. There was sauce and noodles everywhere, but my parents didn't care. They just laughed and snapped photos."

"Sounds like a fun childhood."

"It was the best. I miss those days." Her voice cracked as

her shoulders stiffened. "My dad was the best. I miss him every single day."

I opened my mouth to ask her what happened but closed it when I remembered I had a way of making an ass out of myself around her. As if sensing my discomfort and curiosity, she answered my unspoken question for me.

"He passed last year from a heart attack, which I'm sure you already heard about since he and my mom had lived here for a few years before it happened. Completely unexpected and no history of heart problems in our family."

"I'm so sorry for your loss."

"Thank you. It was hard on my family but hit my mom the worst. She was diagnosed with early-onset dementia shortly after it happened. It's progressed quickly. That's why I decided to move here, so I could take care of her."

My heart melted seeing the love in her eyes for her family.

"Anyway, you didn't ask to get bombarded with sad stories, so let's move on," she said with a forced laugh, turning away so I couldn't see the sadness flashing across her face.

Without thinking, I grabbed her elbow, gently turning her back to face me. Her breath caught in her throat as I pulled her against me, meaning to offer a sympathetic hug but not realizing the amount of chemistry pulling between us the second I touched her.

"I would gladly stand here for hours listening to you tell me the story behind each of these photos," I said softly, inhaling the light scent of jasmine that floated between us.

She licked her lips and looked up at me, something changing in her eyes as her breasts pushed slightly into my chest.

"There you go. That's what I'm talking about. You gotta work for it," Paisley said, startling me for the third time.

Calli immediately pulled back, breaking the connection between us.

"That's not—" I started before she cut me off.

"I know, I know. *That's not what I'm doing.*" She rolled her eyes playfully while balancing a basket of wrapped silverware on her hip. "Just be sure to take some time fixing that leak. Her pipes are *really tight,* if you know what I mean. A little bit of lube should have her up and running again."

"Paisley!" Calli hissed, her cheeks flushing a beautiful shade of red.

"What?" Paisley shrugged and grinned like the cat who ate the canary before returning to the dining area and leaving us alone again.

"I'm so sorry about that," Calli murmured, covering her face.

"Don't worry about it. Fixing pipes is my specialty."

I watched as another wave of crimson washed over her as she picked up on the innuendo I had been brave enough to put down.

# <u>Six</u>

## Calli

Watching the muscles move in Dylan's back as he leaned in and dipped his head under the sink sent waves of heat through my core. I wasn't sure if it was from all the sexual innuendos that had been flying around before he got started or if it was because those same innuendos made me think of the only time I had ever watched porn in my life. It was Paisley's idea, and the quality was as terrible as the acting, but it had a plumber, and he was definitely there to fix a different set of pipes.

I leaned against the wall out of his way and watched, trying to push down the desire to rush over and jump on him. He was a person—not a piece of meat. However, he would be one satisfying piece of meat if I said so myself.

He pulled out and wiped the sweat from his brow with the bottom of his shirt, revealing the most perfect and glorious abs I had ever seen. How was that even possible? I wanted to reach out and drag my nails along the ridges.

"Sorry," he mumbled, as if the sight of his hot, sweaty body was something to apologize for.

"Don't be."

"It gets hot working in small spaces."

"I bet it does," Paisley called from the hallway, but I wasn't sure that Dylan had heard her.

"You can take your shirt off," I offered, immediately second-guessing it.

He gave me a lopsided grin as he climbed up and stood across from me.

"Do you want me to take my shirt off?"

"She does," Paisley answered for me, this time grabbing Dylan's attention.

Instead of being irritated with our little eavesdropping friend, he seemed to find it amusing.

He lifted a brow, silently asking again.

"It's whatever makes you comfortable. You're hot with or without it."

I pressed the palm of my hand to my forehead.

"I mean, it's going to be hot either way. The air conditioning doesn't work back here, and I haven't been able to get anyone out to look at it."

"What's wrong with it?" he asked, tipping his head back to look at the vent.

"I'm not sure. It's a new building, so you would think everything would work fine, but here we are." I shrugged.

"I'll look at it before I go. If I can't figure it out, I'll call my friend to come look at it."

"Oh no, it's okay. You're already doing more than enough with fixing this." I pointed dumbly to the sink.

"It's not a big deal. Besides, he should have made sure it was working in the first place."

"Why's that?"

"Because he owns the company that did the heating and cooling for this building."

"Your friend is Maverick?" I asked, feeling stupid.

He had been around a lot when we were first getting everything set up, and Paisley had practically been drooling over him ever since. We hadn't seen him around town much, but she was nonetheless obsessed with him.

"The one and only."

Before I could say anything more, Paisley came flying around the corner, a flush of heat in her cheeks.

"Did someone say Maverick?"

Dylan gave me a curious look before giving Paisley a smug smile.

"Maybe. Why? Were you listening to our conversation or something?" he teased.

Paisley was one of the kindest people I'd ever known, but she was also the straight-shooter, never turn down a dare kind of girl as well.

"Just making sure you're getting the job done," she replied, tilting her head to the side and making the hair piled on top of her head flop with it.

"Which one?"

"Touché. You got me there. But back to the pressing matter at hand—did someone mention Maverick?"

"I was telling Dylan that it's hot in here because the AC isn't working right. He said he'll look at it, and if he can't fix it, he'll call Maverick to come out."

"No."

Paisley's features changed, her tone more stern.

"You don't want me to look at it?" Dylan asked, folding his arms over his chest.

"I mean, I didn't say that," she stammered. "It's just that you've already taken so much time fixing the sink and taking care of Calli's pipes that it would be rude to tie up your time by having you look at the AC. I think we should just leave it be for now."

"You mean until Maverick comes back?" Dylan questioned, the dimples in his cheeks more prominent with the grin spreading across them.

"Is he coming back? Did he say that? When?"

"You're being strange," I said, eyeing her suspiciously. "What did you do?"

"Nothing." She shook her head, but her eyes told me she was lying.

"Paisley Marie…"

"Ugh, you sound just like Mom," she groaned, leaning against the door frame. "I didn't do anything."

Dylan and I both pinned her with a look but said nothing.

"Fine. I *might have* messed with the vent and shoved a towel up there to block the flow."

"Paisley!" I scolded, desperately trying to hold back my laughter.

"What? You're about to get your pipes fixed. Can't I get some service of my own?"

"You're ridiculous," I laughed, shaking my head.

"You know, you could just ask Maverick for his number," Dylan offered, still grinning.

"I haven't seen him around since he finished up here," she said, pressing her lips into a scowl.

"He's in Fallen Oaks working on a project there, but he'll be back in a few weeks to start the next phase of this development."

"A *few weeks?* That's going to take forever," Paisley groaned, letting her head hang forward.

I heard a heavy sigh from Dylan and looked up to find his fingers flying over the screen of his phone before pressing it to his ear.

"What are you doing?" I asked, an odd excitement flooding through me as he looked at me and his eyes locked on mine.

"Hey, Mav."

"No. Fucking. Way." Paisley's voice was barely above a whisper, but I could see the shock on her face as she watched Dylan.

"Nothing much, just here fixing a leaky pipe at Cravings. Tell your guys to pay better attention next time."

I couldn't hear what was being said on the other end of the line, but Dylan's smirk told me they talked shit to each other often.

"Well, I'm still here at Cravings, and I think you owe Calli and Paisley dinner for your guys fucking up on the job. They're new to town, and you don't want to make a poor impression, do you?"

I started waving my hands no in front of me, but Paisley quickly swatted them away while she hung onto every word Dylan said.

"When are you back in Whiskey Mountain?" He waited a moment while Maverick responded. "Friday? Okay, let me see."

He held the phone away from his face as he looked between Paisley and me.

"Are you ladies free for dinner on Friday?"

"Yes," Paisley squeaked, the excitement almost consuming her.

"Oh, no, I don't think I should be ther—"

"I thought the four of us could go to La Salsa," Dylan said as if reading my mind about not wanting to be a third wheel with Paisley and Maverick.

"Oh. Um. Okay, sure," I stammered as Paisley's nails dug into my hand.

Dylan winked at me, then turned away to continue his conversation while I slapped Paisley's hand away.

"Enough with that, Edward Scissorhands," I scolded, rubbing the skin where her nails had been.

"Sorry! I didn't mean to. I just got so excited!"

"Well then, I feel bad for Maverick if you guys end up in bed together," I teased, knowing it would spur her on.

"I've never had anyone complain yet." She winked.

"Me. I just complained," I joked, following her out of the bathroom to give Dylan time to finish whatever else he had to do. I didn't want to hover, and more importantly, I needed a moment to catch my breath and accept the fact that I was going out with Dylan on Friday night. Whether or not it was supposed to be a date didn't matter because the way he had been looking at me sure made it feel like it was one.

# <u>Seven</u>

## Dylan

"Why am I so fucking nervous?" I muttered, adjusting the collar of my polo shirt that I put on because I felt the need to dress up for dinner with Calli tonight. It wasn't technically a date since Maverick and Paisley would be there, but that didn't damper the thoughts of needing to impress her anyway.

I glanced at the clock, knowing I needed to get out the door before I was late. Again, it wasn't a date, but it would be rude to show up after the girls got there, given that I was the one who had set this whole thing up.

When I pulled into the parking lot of La Salsa, I found Maverick's truck and took the spot next to it. I didn't know what car Calli and Paisley would be in or whether they would even come together. I would have been nervous that they wouldn't have shown up, except that Paisley had practically squeezed the life out of me to say thank you after I hung up with Maverick.

I walked inside and spotted Maverick leaning against a wall, checking something on his phone. I looked around, hoping that we had beaten the girls.

"They're not here yet," Maverick said, not looking up as his fingers flew across the screen. He finished and then shoved it into his pocket.

"Cool," I breathed out and nodded, shoving my hands in my pockets to keep from fidgeting.

"So, wanna tell me what this is all about before they get

here?" His lips turned into a grin, telling me he already knew.

That was Maverick, though. He had an uncanny ability to read people and immediately know what they were thinking. It was also the reason he kept his distance from most women and held his stance against serious relationships. His business was booming, and he didn't have the time for commitment or drama—which, according to him, went hand-in-hand.

"I just thought it would be nice to hang out and have dinner." I shrugged, looking away so he couldn't see the truth in my eyes.

"Which one are you trying to get with?

I could feel his gray eyes penetrating the back of my head as I scanned the room, avoiding the question.

"Given that I've been around both, I would put my money on Calli. I could be wrong, but I'm pretty sure you're not going after Paisley. But if you are, I'll admit that she's probably going to be more than you can handle." He chuckled lightly.

"Isn't that the truth?" I laughed. "She's a fireball. And speaking of which, here they come now."

I nodded to the parking lot, where both girls were climbing out of the back of a car that was dropping them off. Calli looked incredible in a light pink soft, flowy sundress while Paisley was rocking a pair of cutoff jean shorts and a low-cut black lace tank top. I knew from my conversations with Calli that they were best friends, though they couldn't be more different.

"So, am I here for moral support, or what's the game plan?" he asked as they approached the door.

"I have no fucking clue." I tried forcing a smile as they walked through the door, Calli's eyes lighting up the second she spotted me.

"Hey!" she said happily, pulling me in for a hug.

I tried to ignore what was happening in my jeans as she pressed her breasts against my chest, squeezing me tightly.

I could hear Maverick start to laugh before quickly covering it with a cough.

Calli pulled back, her cheeks slightly flushed as she stepped away and smoothed down the front of her dress.

"Sorry, we had a drink before we came, and I tend to get a little *clingy* after a drink or two," she admitted sheepishly.

"Do I make you that nervous?" I asked playfully, keeping my voice low so I didn't embarrass her.

Before she could answer, Paisley spoke for her.

"You do. She thinks you're hot." Paisley chewed her lower lip, satisfaction etched on her face as Calli's face turned beet red.

"Stop pulling that lip between your teeth before I do it for you," Maverick said, nodding to Paisley before stepping behind her. He placed his hand on her lower back to guide her to the line so we could order food.

"Well, if that's the case, I might just bite it even harder," she quipped, giving him a flirty, playful look over her shoulder.

"It starts already," Calli said, walking beside me as we stood behind them. She grinned to let me know she was just teasing.

I waited as the girls placed their orders, nodding for Maverick to go next so I could pay for dinner. I had just been giving him crap about owing the girls dinner and wasn't really going to let him pay.

Once the girls were done, they grabbed their cups and went to the drink station to fill them while we placed our orders. I pulled out my wallet, ready to pay, when Maverick shoved my hand away and shook his head.

"I got it," he informed the girl at the register, who was obviously into him based on the stars in her eyes, like a lovesick puppy.

"Let me get it. It was my idea to do this," I insisted.

He pushed the card across the counter and turned to face me.

"No, it was my guys who messed up the job and you got stuck fixing it. Between the leaky faucet and the AC, I owe you all a meal for that."

I felt my cheeks burn from the smile that split them.

"What?" he asked, taking his card back from the girl after she ran it.

"It turns out that nothing was wrong with the AC. Paisley stuffed a towel up in the vent to block it so she could get you to come back out. The leaky faucet was an easy fix. Don't worry about it."

He shook his head and grinned, looking over to where the girls were watching us from a booth in the corner. Each of them was on opposite sides, which meant that I would sit next to Calli, and Maverick would be next to Paisley. I swallowed hard, my throat suddenly parched as I thought about being in such close proximity to her.

"I'm in for it with her, aren't I?" he questioned, taking the plastic number for our order and heading to the drink station.

"Guess you made quite the impression."

"So it seems." He laughed and filled his cup with ice water while I tried to figure out how I was going to stay cool and not make a complete ass out of myself tonight.

# Eight

## Calli

I lifted the taco to my mouth, trying desperately to take a bite without making a mess. The last thing I wanted was to embarrass myself in front of Dylan by wearing half of my food.

When I'd gotten ready for tonight, I had thrown on a pair of loose shorts and a tank top but was then forced to put on something *cuter* when Paisley showed up and instantly judged my outfit. My mom had agreed with her and even picked the dress that I was wearing. It was her favorite because it had tiny strawberries that were hard to see unless you were really staring at it.

I opted for a comfy pair of flip-flops but was outnumbered once again and had compromised with a pair of wedge sandals that had one strap around my ankle.

I felt nervous being around Dylan outside of work, and even though this wasn't a date, it still didn't feel any less like one. I wanted to get to know him, and maybe if we hung out enough, it would dull that heat that always seemed to blaze through my veins whenever he was around.

"How's your food?" he asked, his voice low while Paisley told Maverick a story about getting chased by a shark when we lived in Miami. She was definitely playing it up and being dramatic about how her life was in danger when, in reality, it was a baby sand shark that she almost killed when she nearly stepped on it. Thankfully, it got away, and neither was hurt in the encounter.

"It's delicious," I replied, wiping my mouth with a napkin as I swallowed my bite. "How's yours?"

He lifted his fajita, the savory aroma of onions and peppers making my mouth water.

"Have a bite," he offered, lifting it toward my lips.

They parted of their own free will, accepting the bite he offered.

I bit down, the taste exploding on my tongue. I closed my eyes as I chewed, a soft moan escaping my lips. I had been to La Salsa plenty of times since moving here, but I had yet to try the fajitas. Now I didn't know how I would ever go back to eating anything else.

My eyelids fluttered open, and I found his eyes locked on me, his jaw tight as he held the fajita in his hand.

"That was delicious," I said softly, lowering my eyes to my plate while the heat flooded my body.

I could tell he wanted to say something, but he didn't. Instead, he lowered his head and took a bite, not bothering to look up when Paisley asked another question that both of us had missed the first time.

"Do you remember that, Calli?" she asked, her tone a little louder to make sure I heard her this time.

"Remember what?"

"That time we went skiing in Aspen and almost got stranded on the mountain?"

"Ugh, that I do." I groaned, remembering the bitter cold that clung to us hours after we figured out our way back down the mountain. "I'll never go skiing with you again."

"Eh, we were fine." Paisley shrugged her shoulders and lifted her fork to her mouth. Everyone else had some sort of fried food on their plate except for her. She'd gone with the taco salad and opted out of the fried tortilla shell—which I'd informed her she was crazy for doing.

Unlike me, Paisley was one of those people who couldn't eat when it was hot outside. She'd settle for a salad and eat as light as she could to avoid feeling sick after. Me, I could eat the heartiest of meals any time of year, which was a trait I got from my mother. It was also why I constantly had to reconsider the menu options at Cravings because not everyone wanted a Salisbury steak and mashed potatoes while they were roasting in the sun.

The conversation continued about the skiing mishap, which turned into a story about Dylan and Maverick snowboarding years ago and wiping out. Maverick had walked away with a few broken ribs, while Dylan broke his leg and had to wear a cast for 12 weeks.

I felt my body start to relax as the night continued, and suddenly it was time to go.

Paisley pulled out her phone and started requesting an Uber when I felt Dylan's body shift next to mine.

"Shit," she muttered, chewing her lip again.

"What's wrong?" I asked.

"It's going to be at least half an hour before we can get a ride." She lowered her phone and looked up at me. "Do you want to call your mo—"

"No," I snapped, a little more aggressively than I meant to. "You know that it's not safe for her to drive this late at night."

"Ok." Paisley set her phone on the table and waited for me to tell her what I wanted to do.

"I can give you a ride home," Dylan offered, looking between us.

"Thank you, but I don't want you to go out of your way."

"There's nothing in Whiskey Mountain that is out of the way," he countered. "Besides, Chuck over there is one of the few Uber drivers I know in town, and he's tossing back his third beer. I don't think you should take one home tonight. Let me drive you guys."

"But we're on opposite sides of town. That would be a lot to ask of you."

"It's not a problem."

"I'm heading to Fallen Oaks," Maverick said. "So, I can take whoever is headed that way."

"That would be me," Paisley said, beaming up at him.

"Then it looks like you're stuck with me," Dylan said, bumping his shoulder with mine.

*Stuck* wasn't how I would have put it.

# Nine

## Dylan

My mouth had a way of talking itself into situations that my brain wasn't prepared for. Like when I first set up the double date tonight and now with driving Calli home. She sat beside me, bouncing her head and tapping her feet to the song on the radio while I tried to maintain my grip on the steering wheel with sweaty palms.

I pulled into her driveway and cut the engine. I didn't look over at her, just kept my eyes straight ahead with my hands still gripping the leather of the steering wheel while I tried to figure out what to say.

"Tonight was fun. Thank you," she said, breaking the silence for me.

She unbuckled her seatbelt and turned toward me, a loose curl bouncing free from her ponytail before she tucked it behind her ear. I wanted to reach over and do it for her, to feel the soft touch of her skin.

"Thank you for coming. It was fun to hang out for a bit."

I sounded like a robot, everything coming out like preprogrammed responses that lacked any emotion to them.

"I would invite you in, but my mom might be up and—"

"It's not a problem. Really," I blurted out.

She reached over and gently squeezed my hand, getting my attention before her eyes landed on mine.

"Maybe we can hang out again soon? Just the two of us?" she offered.

"Like a date?" I asked before I could stop myself.

Her lips twitched as a smile spread across her face.

"Do you want it to be a date?"

"Fuck yeah I do," I rushed out, feeling a warmth spread through me as her grin widened.

"Well, then, it's a date." She laughed, then let go of my hand as she leaned in and kissed my cheek. "Does tomorrow night work for you?"

I knew Saturday nights were reserved for hanging out with Ramona and Maggie, but I also didn't want to say no to Calli. It wasn't like the girls hadn't canceled on me before so they could hang out with their boyfriends instead, yet this left me feeling guilty. Way too guilty.

"I, um, I have this thing—" I started but stopped when my phone started ringing. The Bluetooth in my truck picked up, showing Maggie's name on the screen.

"Sorry," I apologized, reaching to press the button to decline the call.

"Don't be. It's totally fine. I gotta get inside to check on my mom, but call me tomorrow and we can figure out a day that works."

She passed a piece of paper she pulled from her purse to me and opened the door. I opened mine and rushed around to help her out, frustrated that I hadn't gotten there in time to open the door for her.

"Such a gentleman," she said, taking my hand as I guided her down.

I ignored the way her dress rode high on her thighs, inches

of skin begging to be touched.

Once she was out, I leaned in for a hug, more used to doing it with Maggie and Ramona than actually expecting to give her one.

But she didn't seem to mind as she wrapped her arms around my neck and lifted on her tiptoes. Her lips gently brushed against mine, planting the softest kiss on them. I kissed her back, trying to reign in the urge to lower my hands to her ass and plunge my tongue inside her mouth.

She giggled as if knowing what I was thinking.

Her hand came around and cupped my face as she tilted her head and deepened the kiss. Her lips parted, inviting me in.

I groaned as my cock stiffened between us, desperate to get under her dress.

"I'll talk to you tomorrow," she said breathlessly as she pulled away and placed her hand on my chest as we separated.

"Tomorrow," I repeated, already missing the feel of her lips on mine.

She turned and walked to the door, throwing one last look over her shoulder as she chewed her lip and went inside.

I climbed into my truck and found the piece of paper she left with her phone number on it, then quickly programmed it into my phone so I didn't lose it.

I sent a quick text message, letting her know it was me. I set my phone down and started the truck when Maggie called again. I pressed the accept button and backed out of the driveway so I didn't look like a weirdo for hanging out there.

"Hey," I said, my tone reflecting the high I currently felt.

"Hey, you," she replied with a laugh. "Someone is in a good mood tonight. What's going on?"

"Nothing," I lied, pulling up to a stop sign.

"Didn't he have that double date tonight?" Ramona offered, her voice further away than Maggie's, which meant I was on speakerphone.

"That's right!" Maggie squealed. "How was it? Did you fall in love?"

"Stop it," Ramona scolded playfully. "Not everyone *loves love* the way you do. Plus, how could he fall in love tonight when he was already head over heels in love with her *before* they went out?"

"I'm hanging up," I joked.

"No, you're not," Maggie said. "You love us, and you know it."

"There's a whole lot of the word *love* floating around tonight. You know it makes me get all itchy when I hear it."

"Oh, whatever. Knock it off or I'm going to hack into Maggie's blog and tell the world how much you love love and that you're in love with Calli."

I knew that Ramona was likely playing, but then again, there was a good chance she wasn't. Her fiancé was also a technology God, so there wasn't anything I wouldn't put past her at this point.

"Was there a reason for this call, or was it just to harass me?" I asked, turning on my signal to turn onto Main Street.

"Of course there was," Maggie laughed. "We wanted to see if you wanted to do lunch tomorrow instead of dinner. I'm heading out of town for a few days with Owen, and Ramona needs to do inventory."

"Yeah, lunch works."

I breathed a sigh of relief that I could meet up with Calli tomorrow night, after all, without having to cancel on my friends.

"Perfect! How about Whiskey's at 11?" Maggie asked. "We can go for brunch."

"I'll be there," I replied at the same time that Ramona confirmed she would be there too. There would be bacon and mimosas—two of the easiest ways to summon Ramona somewhere if you didn't have Cool Ranch Doritos.

I ended the call and headed home, desperate to talk to Calli again.

# Ten

## Calli

Mom was already asleep when I got home, so I made my way quietly to the kitchen and made a cup of chamomile tea. I was still wound up from that kiss with Dylan and needed something to help calm me so I could sleep tonight.

I knew his mouth would be magical just from how his full lips moved when he talked, but I never imagined they would leave me so breathless and desperate for more. I was a lady, so I had walked away and said goodnight, but part of me wanted to be like one of those girls in the romance books I read. They would have hiked up their dress and bent over the hood of the car as they got fucked into oblivion. Lucky bitches.

The tea kettle whistled at the same time that my phone dinged with a new text message alert. I moved the kettle to a trivet and turned off the stove while my fingers quickly raced across the screen to unlock it.

**Unknown: Hey, this is Dylan. I saved your number in my phone.**

**Unknown: Thank you again for tonight. It was fun.**

My cheeks split as I quickly added his contact info to my phone and texted him back.

**Me: I saved yours too.**

**Me: Thank you for inviting me. Can't wait to see you again soon!**

The text messages he had sent were from fifteen minutes ago, so I didn't expect him to be on his phone or to respond right away to mine. I poured the water into a mug, letting the tea steep when I heard the ding again.

**Dylan: My plans for tomorrow changed, and I'm now free tomorrow night if you still wanted to hang out. If not, that's cool too.**

**Me: Tomorrow night is perfect. Is there anything you'd like to do?**

**Dylan: I'm up for whatever as long as I get to spend time with you.**

I placed a hand over my heart as it fluttered in my chest.

**Me: I was going to say the same thing.**

**Dylan: How about dinner? I can make a reservation somewhere if you'd like. We don't have a ton of fine dining options in Whiskey Mountain, but there are a few in Fallen Oaks if that's not too far for you.**

I chewed my lip nervously, debating whether or not to be so bold.

Fuck it.

**Me: Dinner sounds great, but I'd really rather do something lowkey instead, if that's okay?**

**Dylan: Absolutely.**

**Me: I don't want to be too forward, but since it's hard to cook for you here without having an extra guest during our date, I thought maybe I could cook for you at your house.**

**Me: You can say no. I don't want to make you uncomfortable.**

**Me: I just haven't quite gotten used to small-town life and everyone watching what you do when you go out.**

**I miss being able to just be me and not have to worry about being the talk of the town.**

**Dylan: You don't have to cook for me, Calli. I can try to cook, or we can order in.**

**Me: I love cooking. It's my stress reliever and cooking for people brings me a lot of joy.**

**Dylan: Can I at least buy the groceries?**

I pulled the teabag out of the mug and set it on the saucer before taking a sip.

**Me: Thank you, but I got it. I like to decide what I'm making while I'm at the store, so it would be hard to give you a list.**

I waited a few minutes for him to reply. I knew he didn't want to let me do the cooking, but it was such a soothing thing for me.

Finally, he responded.

**Dylan: Alright. But I'm getting the wine and dessert.**

**Me: Deal.**

**Dylan: See you at my house around 7?**

**Me: Text me the address, and I'll be there.**

A few minutes later, one final text message came through with his address and a smiley emoji. I took the empty mug to the sink and headed to my bedroom, my brain racing a mile a minute as I thought about what I would make for dinner tomorrow night.

# Eleven

## Dylan

Whiskey's was already packed by the time I got there. Thankfully the girls beat me and had snagged one of the last tables in the back.

"Sorry, there was an accident on Main Street," I explained, bending down to hug each of them. "Did you guys already order?"

I figured they would have, given that Ramona gets hangry quickly.

"We did. And we took the liberty of ordering for you, too," Ramona replied with a smile.

"How do you know what I want?" I pulled out the chair and sat down between them.

"Because you always get the same thing and have never once ordered anything different," Maggie said with a laugh. "French toast with a side of bacon and sourdough toast."

I grinned and nodded my head. She was right; I never deviated once I found something I liked.

"So, how was last night?" Maggie asked, immediately jumping in.

"It was fine," I replied, lowering my head as I adjusted the seat beneath me while avoiding their curious looks.

"Just fine?" Ramona pressed.

"Yeah." I shrugged.

"You had dinner with Calli, and it was *just fine*?" Her eyes narrowed as she waited for me to give in and elaborate.

That was the difference between Maggie and Ramona. Maggie was kinder and would back off until I was ready to talk about something, whereas Ramona would stab me if I didn't speak fast enough for her liking.

"It wasn't just Calli and me, remember? Maverick and Paisley were there too. It wasn't a date, just dinner with friends. I drove Calli home last night. It wasn't a big deal."

My cheeks flushed with heat as I remembered our kiss and I knew that I had just given myself away. Ramona and Maggie's eyebrows shot up as they studied me, wondering what I was withholding.

"Spill it," Ramona demanded, pointing a finger at me as a waitress arrived with our food. She set the plates down and promised to be back in a few minutes with the mimosas the girls had ordered. Once she was out of earshot, Ramona pressed harder. "Now."

I sighed heavily, feeling my shoulders rise and fall with my breath.

"Fine. She asked to hang out again and we have a *date* tonight."

"A date?!" Maggie squealed, clapping her hands excitedly. "Dyl! I'm so excited and happy for you!"

"Thanks," I said quietly, trying to avoid drawing more attention to our table.

The waitress returned with three mimosas, then scurried off to another table that was waiting to place their order.

"Nope. That's not all of it," Ramona said, her nostrils slightly flaring.

She had her food now, so she could technically eat and calm the fury raging inside, but that still didn't stop me from scanning the room for a bag of Cool Ranch Doritos. Usually, I could toss one her way and then run while she was distracted.

"Is there more?" Maggie asked with a tinge of hope in her voice.

I glared at Ramona and then turned to Maggie.

"We might have kissed."

I closed my eyes as Maggie squealed and Ramona fisted the air, talking about how she knew it.

We got a few looks from people at the other tables, but they turned and minded their own business when they saw it was just us. Apparently, this was the type of behavior the people in Whiskey Mountain expected of me and my friends.

"Oh my gosh!! I can't believe it! When are you going to see her again?" Maggie asked, still clapping excitedly.

"Tonight. She's coming to my place to cook dinner since she's living with her mom."

"You're letting her cook for you on your first official date?" Ramona questioned, brows pulled together as her breakfast burrito hung inches from her mouth.

"I offered to take her to dinner. To go somewhere where we had to make a reservation. Hell, I even offered to go to Fallen Oaks for dinner. But she didn't want to do any of that. She said that she just wanted to stay in and that she wanted to cook."

"You should treat her. It's the first date," Ramona continued.

"I agree, but I'm also listening to her and trying to make this about what *she* wants. I told her I'll take care of the wine and dessert."

"Do you know what she's making?" Maggie asked.

"No, she hasn't told me. I offered to buy the groceries, but she said no because she likes to pick stuff while she's at the store and figure out dinner there."

"Then how will you know what kind of wine to get if you don't know what you're having?" Ramona took a bite and then wiped her mouth while waiting for a response.

"I was planning to get a bottle of red and a bottle of white. Then I should be covered regardless of what she makes."

"What about dessert?" Ramona attempted to cover her mouth as she spoke but it was too full, so the words came out kind of muffled.

"I haven't decided yet."

I felt Maggie's eyes on me and knew she was up to something.

"What about banana nut muffins?" she offered. "I can whip up a batch so you have some fresh ones for tonight. Or I can call the store and see if there's any left, but I don't want you to take something that has been sitting out for a few hours."

"I'm good, but thank you."

"Oh, come on! They would be the *perfect* dessert for tonight! And did you know they have health benefits— especially for the guys? They increase—"

"Maggie, I'm begging you to stop right there. I appreciate you trying to help, but the last thing that I need for my date tonight is to remember that you made a dessert that can improve my stamina."

She shrugged and pressed her lips together.

"I'm just saying it's never hurt anyone. Owen doesn't complain—"

"Nope. None of that. I'm trying to eat my breakfast before Ramona calls dibs on it, so no more talking about food and their sexual benefits, please."

Maggie tipped her head back and laughed while Ramona blatantly eyed my plate. I stabbed a piece of French toast with my fork just to make sure she didn't get any more ideas.

# Twelve

## Calli

A wave of blonde curls clouded my vision as I bent over, picking up the cucumber I had dropped. I still had no idea what I was making for dinner, but I had to figure it out and fast because I was expected at Dylan's house in half an hour.

I put the rogue vegetable back in its bin and rounded the corner. It was freaking hot outside, so I didn't want to make anything heavy, but then again, making a simple salad didn't exactly scream *romantic date*.

I chewed my nail as I roamed the produce section, looking for anything that called out and gave me ideas. But instead of a vegetable calling to me, Paisley did instead.

"You look lost," she commented, her brows pulling together as she watched me lower my hand from my mouth.

"I'm trying to figure out what to make for dinner tonight."

"Frozen pizza. There. Done. Problem solved."

I rolled my eyes and shook my head.

"I'm not taking a frozen pizza," I laughed, walking along the other side of the produce section, disappointed with the quality.

"Taking? Where are you going?"

I chewed my lip nervously, picking up an eggplant and studying it before putting it down and turning to look at her.

"I'm making dinner at Dylan's tonight."

"You're making dinner?"

"Yeah, it's our first date," I answered sheepishly.

"He's making you cook on your first date?" she asked in disbelief.

"He's not making me do anything. He offered to take me to dinner, somewhere nice with reservations. But I asked him if we could stay in and have dinner at his place. I love cooking, and I think it will be nice to hang out and not have to worry about nosey people watching us."

She folded her arms over her chest, her shopping basket jutting out oddly at her side.

"What?" I laughed nervously and walked over to the fruit section. This wasn't helpful unless I was going to make a fruit salad, but I needed the distraction from her right now.

"What exactly are you planning to do that you don't want people seeing?" She wiggled her eyebrows suggestively.

"Nothing," I laughed again, but it sounded more fake this time because it was. I would be lying if I said that I hadn't been thinking about *all* the things that might happen at Dylan's house tonight.

"Let me guess, you're gonna play it off tomorrow as *nothing happened; it was just an innocent kiss*, and then withhold all of the dirty details from me."

"We technically already kissed," I said, grinning.

"When?!"

"Last night when he took me home. But it really was just a kiss, nothing more."

"I can tell that you wanted it to be, though."

"Me and him both," I laughed. "I could feel *everything* through my dress, and even though he tried to hide it, it was still there and *very obvious*."

"So then, is tonight going to be… you know? Wink, wink."

"I don't know," I giggled. "It's not like it's premeditated or anything."

"Well, all I can say is that if you hold his balls the way you're holding those plums, you have nothing to worry about."

I gasped and looked down at the plums I was cradling in my hand, conveniently right between my boobs.

"Oh my God!" I shrieked, dropping them back into their section. "What is wrong with me?"

"Relax." She laughed, locking her arm into mine. "You always make a killer Caprese pasta salad. Why not make that with some grilled chicken?"

"Have I ever told you how much I love you?" I looked up at her, batting my eyes.

"Yes, and I know you'll love me even more if I help you shop. So let's go."

Paisley and I scampered off to grab the stuff I needed for dinner, rushing to make it to Dylan's on time.

By the time I got there, I was a few minutes late, but he didn't seem to mind when he opened the door and insisted on taking the grocery bags from me.

I was nervous being at his house, but the second that I walked in, all of that faded away when I smelled the soft scent of vanilla floating through the air. He set the groceries on the kitchen island, then took my hand and gave me a tour of the house.

It was nice and the complete opposite of what I imagined a "bachelor pad" to look like. Instead of mess and clutter everywhere, each room was clean and organized, with paintings on the walls and framed family photos in the hallway.

We made our way back to the kitchen, and I could tell he didn't want to let go of my hand any more than I wanted him to.

"What can I help with?" he asked, looking incredibly delicious in a gray graphic t-shirt with cargo shorts. He was the perfect combination of comfy and sexy, though I wasn't sure he knew it. Most guys were super cocky when they knew they were attractive, but Dylan wasn't one of them.

"Do you have a grill?" I asked, looking up at him as I pulled stuff out of the bag.

"I do."

"Do you know how to use it?" I teased, remembering that he said he wasn't a good cook.

"That's pretty much the only thing I know how to use." He laughed.

"Perfect. Can you grill these without burning them" I arched an eyebrow as I held them out to him, refusing to hand them over until he agreed.

"Yes, I can grill them without burning them."

He took the package from me and then scrunched his face.

"Do you have a backup plan, though? Just in case?"

I opened my mouth to tell him not to worry about it but caught the wink he gave me and shook my head instead.

"Alright, Grill Master. Go do your thing so I can do mine," I teased.

"Holler if you need anything," he called on his way out the sliding glass door to the grill outback.

I nodded and took a deep breath, trying to shake off the nerves so *I* didn't end up being the one who ruined dinner.

# Thirteen

## Dylan

"You had one job," she teased, covering her mouth to keep from laughing as we stared at the black chicken on the grill.

"I know," I groaned, sliding a hand down my face.

"How did it happen?" She giggled. "I've never met anyone who's burned food on a grill."

"I have. I grew up with a guy who could burn anything. Wanted to be a chef when he grew up."

"Aww. So, what happened? Did he learn to cook and go on to be a chef?"

I turned to look at her and shook my head.

"The opposite. He became a firefighter. Probably a useful skill since he still catches everything on fire."

"Oh my God!" Her hands flew up to her mouth to hide her laughter as a snort erupted. "You're kidding, right?"

"Nope. True story. He lives in Beaumont Creek now. Still a terrible cook, but a decent firefighter," I joked, remembering that I needed to check in and see how Jones was doing. The last time I talked to him, he had caught cinnamon rolls on fire at the fire station.

"Wow. That's crazy. Poor guy."

I nodded and poked the chicken with a fork. It wasn't just burnt—it was burned to a crisp, and it was hard to tell what it was supposed to be.

Now it wasn't technically my fault that I burned it. I had been grilling since I was a teenager and my dad trusted me not to set the backyard on fire. But I had never had to grill while watching a beautiful woman cook inside my kitchen.

Things were going fine for a bit as I watched Calli move around as if she had been in my kitchen a thousand times. It was when she reached up to grab something out of the cabinet, and her sundress rose so high I could almost see her ass cheeks that did me in.

I shook my head and cleared it, trying to get out of the trance she had me in so I *didn't* burn the food. But then after I flipped the chicken, she bent over the sink, washing something in the colander she had found, and I was a goner.

Her dress rode up again, this time giving me that glimpse of her ass that I so desperately wanted. Given the amount of skin I saw without any panty lines, I assumed she was wearing a thong. I couldn't look away if I tried, my cock hardening almost instantly.

"Well, we have pasta salad and bread," Calli said, interrupting the train of thought that was leading into dangerous territory.

"Sounds perfect."

"There's no protein," she laughed, "but I think we'll make do without it. Are you ready to eat?"

She looked up at me, her blue eyes sparkling under her thick dark lashes.

"I'm more than ready to eat," I said, noticing the curious glance she gave me before heading inside.

I hadn't meant for it to come out that way, but then again, I hadn't meant to think about eating her when I answered.

We sat at the kitchen table, and Calli filled two bowls with the pasta salad before placing a basket of bread between us. I poured the wine while she finished getting everything ready, then we dove in.

The food was amazing but dull compared to the woman sitting across from me. Every time she talked, I watched her face light up, her lips plump and beautiful with each word she spoke. I didn't say much, just let her keep talking because I was mesmerized by her.

We finished dinner and then moved to the living room, sitting close enough on the couch where I could feel the heat coming from her body but far enough apart that I was able to refrain from reaching over and touching her.

"Do you want to watch a movie?" I asked. "Or we can play a game. I have a lot of board games. You can take your pick."

I snapped my mouth shut to keep from rambling again. I was nervous, and I knew she could tell.

"Well, while I love a good movie, I think it would be fun to play a game. What are the options?"

She grinned, and I smiled back, relaxing a little.

I got up and walked to the entertainment center to read them to her.

"We've got Monopoly, Scrabble, Clue, Battleship, and Twister."

Her grin widened as she leaned forward, mischief dancing on her face.

"Twister. Definitely gotta go with Twister."

"You sure?" I asked before taking it off the shelf. She was wearing a dress, and I could only imagine what would happen if we found ourselves in a tangled mess on the floor.

"Oh, I'm sure."

I pressed my lips together to keep from saying anything stupid and grabbed the game.

Since she was my guest and it was her idea to play Twister, I let her spin first.

"Right foot red," she announced, handing me the spinner while she put her foot on the red circle closest to the edge.

I flicked the spinner and watched as it spun around, landing in a spot that would put me in a hell of a predicament.

"Left hand blue." I offered an apologetic smile as I stood beside her and bent down, placing my left hand on the blue space beside her foot. My head was so close to her ass that I had to resist the urge to lean over and bite it.

Just a little nip. That was all that I needed.

She took the spinner and waited for it to land on her next move.

"Left hand yellow."

Her cheeks flushed as she handed me the spinner before leaning across and bending over to put her left hand on the yellow circle. Her ass popped right up in front of my face as she did.

*Don't bite it.*

I placed the spinner on the floor and used my right hand to spin it.

"Right foot red." *Fuck. How the hell was I supposed to play this game without thinking about all of the positions we could do it in?*

I stood up as much as I could, still keeping my left hand on the blue circle while trying to get my right foot on one of the red circles. I somehow maneuvered, but not without lining my pelvis up against her ass.

My cock stiffened right away, and the small gasp that

escaped her throat confirmed that she felt it.

"We can stop if you want," I offered, not wanting her to be uncomfortable.

"Why? Are you afraid I'll win?" she asked, taking the spinner from me and placing it on the floor. She spun with her one free hand, and we watched as it stopped.

"Right hand blue," she said quietly.

She passed it back to me, then moved herself to get in position to have her right hand on the blue circle while her left stayed on the yellow. She was bent over even further, her dress riding dangerously high as her ass pressed harder into my groin.

I inhaled slowly and deeply, praying that the oxygen would rush back to my brain. I wasn't sure if it was just me that felt this game taking a sudden sexual twist, but I didn't want to be an ass and overstep if she hadn't intended for it to turn this way.

Right as I was about to spin, her phone rang.

I stilled momentarily, not wanting to knock her over if she needed to go get it. Her body had tensed almost immediately when she heard it.

"Do you want to get that?" I asked.

"I probably should. That's my mom's ringtone. I have it set to something different so I know when she calls."

I stepped back, extending my hand to help her up. She took it and smiled, tucking a strand of hair behind her ear after it popped out of her ponytail.

Wanting to give her some space, I went to the kitchen and filled a glass with ice water to cool me off while she talked to her mom.

# Fourteen

## Calli

Who knew their mom could be an accidental cock-block?

Things had started getting pretty hot and heavy with Dylan and me as we played Twister. I could feel the way his body reacted to mine every time we touched. There was a chemistry there that was almost as palpable as the cock that poked me in the butt when I bent over to put my hand on the blue circle.

I knew there was a good chance that playing the game while wearing a dress would result in some heavy foreplay, if not sex, but I was fully on board with it. Dylan seemed slightly relieved when my mom called and interrupted us, so maybe it was for the better. I could tell he was interested in me, but I didn't want to make him uncomfortable if we took things too fast.

I finished the phone call and assured my mom I would be home later. Paisley was hanging out there tonight so I didn't have to worry about Mom, but that didn't mean she wouldn't call me repeatedly to see where I was.

"Sorry about that," I apologized, setting my phone down on the coffee table as I sat beside Dylan on the couch. "My mom freaks out sometimes if she doesn't remember where I'm at."

"Don't apologize. She should always come first. How's she doing?"

I shrugged, letting a heavy breath out.

"She's okay I guess. When I first moved out here, she

had just been diagnosed, and it was really mild. But she's struggling a lot lately with remembering things that happen. She's comfortable being at home where things feel familiar, but when I take her to the restaurant with me, sometimes she freaks out because she doesn't remember where she is. She has no idea that I moved here and opened a restaurant or that she helps me run the kitchen."

"That has to be hard," he said softly, his hand gently brushing mine.

"It is. But I think the hardest part is when she asks for my dad. It breaks my heart every single time and I don't have it in me to tell her he died. I re-live the grief and heartbreak every time we have the conversation. Her doctor said not to tell her he's dead, but she gets so obsessive about where he is that she has a panic attack, and I have no choice but to tell her."

My eyes filled with tears as I blinked quickly to force them away.

Dylan reached over and pulled me into his side, wrapping a protective arm around my shoulder.

"I'm sorry, this is so embarrassing," I muttered against his chest as he passed me a tissue.

I wiped my eyes and blew my nose, hating that I was falling apart on our first date.

"There's nothing embarrassing about you being human and having emotions, Calli."

"No, but I'm sitting here getting snot all over your shirt. There's nothing sexy about that," I snorted.

He pulled away slightly, and I was mortified that he was checking his shirt to look for said snot trails.

His eyes roamed my features, taking me in from head to toe as I found comfort in their earthy brown depths.

"You could wear a clown costume, and I would still think

you're sexy."

I pulled my head back, slightly taken aback by his statement.

"What?" I laughed, my stomach shaking as it started to consume me. "You think clowns are sexy?"

"Not all clowns. But you as a clown? Fuck yeah."

"You mean like me wearing nothing but a red nose, right?"

"I'll take all of it, Calli. The red nose. Giant shoes. Shit, you could pull a rabbit out of your ass, and I would be both impressed and probably turned on because I got to see your ass."

I laughed so hard my stomach hurt.

"I might know a few tricks, but I can guarantee that I will not be pulling any rabbits out of my ass."

*Not even the vibrating kind.*

He reached over and pulled me closer, nestling my head under his chin as I laid on his chest.

"While I would love to see what tricks you've got, my point is that there's nothing about you that I wouldn't find sexy. I'm glad that you feel comfortable enough around me to let your walls down and be vulnerable. Taking care of someone who needs your help is a lot, and I admire how you've stepped up for your mom. You're an amazing woman, Calli. Someone to admire, not be embarrassed about."

I tipped my head up and looked at him, wondering how in the world I'd found someone as sweet as him.

# Fifteen

## Dylan

Dinner with Calli went better than I imagined, mainly because I had expected to make a fool of myself and scare her off before we even had dessert. We talked for a bit, had a little more wine, ate chocolate-covered strawberries on the deck while watching for shooting stars, and flirted shamelessly. It was the perfect night and I couldn't wait to see her again.

The week passed by at a mind-numbingly slow pace, each day dragging on worse than the one before. We were finishing up the rest of the shopping center, so I didn't get to see Calli much, given that her section was already complete and we were moving to the other side. Not only that, but Cravings had gotten a fresh wave of new customers which resulted in a constant line out the door.

We'd texted a few times once we were home and winding down from the day, but it wasn't the same as seeing her and watching her face as her features changed with every story she told. If she didn't own a successful restaurant, I would have thought she would be the perfect storyteller for kids because she was always so animated when she spoke, and it was impossible not to watch her.

I packed up my stuff and was glad to call it a day. It was Friday, which was the start of the weekend for most, but for me, it was date night with Calli.

She'd been stressed this week with her mom not doing as well as she had been before. I suggested doing something at her house, but she was worried that I would be uncomfortable spending our time together with her mom. I informed her that she was being silly and confirmed that I would be over at 6:30, the time her mother ate dinner every night.

I rushed home and showered before heading to the store to grab a few things to take to Calli's. My mom always taught me that it was rude to show up to dinner at someone's house empty-handed, but I didn't know what they were making, so it was hard to decide what to contribute.

I grabbed a bottle of sweet tea, knowing that Calli had mentioned it was her mom's favorite, and skipped the wine tonight. It was going to be another hot night, so I grabbed some ice cream cones and a fresh watermelon, remembering another of her mom's favorites.

When I got to her house, I balanced the shopping bag on one arm while I held onto the bouquets. I rang the doorbell, hoping I didn't startle her mom if she opened the door. Thankfully, Calli grabbed it instead, her eyes wide at the sight of the flowers.

"Dylan," she whispered, leaning around to see me past the massive bouquets.

"These are for you," I said, separating the ones I'd picked for her. "I wasn't sure what your favorite flower was, but I got these because they're vibrant and beautiful, just like you. I also added some calla lilies because they sounded like Calli." I shrugged and felt my cheeks prickle with embarrassment.

She lifted the flowers to her nose, breathing them in as she held the door open for me to come inside.

I expected the house to be less modernly decorated, given how old it was, but I was pleasantly surprised by the tile floors and gray walls. There were pops of color here and there with a random piece of art, but other than that, everything was clean and very minimalist.

"I got these for your mom," I said, following her into the

kitchen and setting the bags down. "I remembered you saying that daisies were her favorite."

"They are my favorite," a voice behind me said.

I turned around to find Patti standing behind me. Seeing her and Calli together in the same room made my head spin with how much they looked alike.

"Thank you, Dylan. That was very kind of you." She leaned in for a hug and kissed my cheek as she took the flowers from me. "How are your parents?"

"They're doing well," I said, smiling. "It's nice to see you. Thank you for allowing me to join you ladies for dinner."

She smiled, and I saw the relief on Calli's face.

"I wasn't sure what to bring, so I grabbed a few things." I opened the grocery bag and began pulling stuff out. "I figured no matter what we're having, you can never go wrong with sweet tea. And since it's so hot outside, I grabbed some ice cream and watermelon to cool us off after dinner."

"That's so kind of you. Thank you." Calli's eyes started to water again, but she looked away before her mom noticed. "I'll take the ice cream to the freezer so it doesn't melt. Mom, do you want to fix everyone a glass of tea? Dinner should be ready in a few minutes."

"Of course, dear," Patti said, giving her daughter's hand a quick pat before walking to the cabinets next to the sink. Calli mouthed *thank you* as she walked past to take the ice cream to the deep freezer in the garage.

I was about to offer to help Patti when I saw her opening and closing all of the cabinet doors, sighing heavily in frustration. I stepped closer, unsure of what the problem was but not wanting to upset her.

"Can I help with anything?" I offered, my voice soft and gentle.

"I can't find a damn thing in this house anymore. I'm looking for the glasses with the blue geese at the bottom. Where's Charlie? He'll know what I'm talking about."

My words froze in my throat, unable to say anything.

"Dad's not here, Mom," Calli said, placing her arm around her mom's shoulders. "And we don't have the glasses with the blue geese anymore. You sold them when I was in kindergarten because you said they creeped you out."

Patti blinked her eyes a few times, seeming lost and disoriented.

"I did?"

"Yeah, but then you got the ones with pink hearts. You said they reminded you of Valentine's Day, which was also your and Dad's anniversary."

"Where is he? Is he coming home soon?"

"No, Mama. Daddy isn't coming home. Why don't I fix you a glass of sweet tea?"

She led her to the table in the dining room and pulled out a chair, helping her in before joining me in the kitchen again.

"I'm sorry about that," she apologized, opening the cabinet door before I reached up and closed it.

Her eyes snapped to mine, concern etched on her face.

I reached out and gently grabbed her waist, pulling her close to me.

"You do not get to apologize to me again tonight. Okay?"

She lowered her eyes, so I lifted her chin with my finger until she was looking at me again.

"I mean it, Calli. No more apologizing when you haven't done anything wrong. Nor has your mom. I'm here because I want to be, and I'm more than honored that you're letting me into this part of your life. I want to help; I just need you to tell me how. You're not in this alone, I promise."

Her lip trembled as she fought off the emotion that wanted to overcome her.

"Okay," she whispered. "Usually, she's better after we eat. She needs some time without being pushed into anything. I try not to bring up anything from the past which might upset her. Right now, she won't remember anything that's happened recently. So I let her guide the conversation and keep it as stress-free for her as possible."

"Got it," I replied softly. "You lead the way, and I'll follow. And Calli, if you need me to go, just say the word. I won't be offended by any means. I want to make your mom as comfortable as possible, and if my presence upsets her, I don't want to do that."

"Let's just see how it goes. I've learned that I never know what to expect, so I try to roll with the punches."

She smiled and leaned up to kiss my cheek. We both went about getting dinner ready while Patti sat at the dining room table sipping her sweet tea.

I helped Calli carry the dishes in and set them on the trivets on the table. Patti's eyes lit up when she noticed the casserole dish.

"Is that meatloaf?" she asked, leaning in and taking a deep breath.

"It is." Calli smiled down at her mom as she served some with mashed potatoes.

"Is it my birthday?" Patti asked, lifting her fork but stopping while she waited for an answer. "Charlie always makes me meatloaf for my birthday."

She smiled brightly; so much hope filled her eyes.

"Yes, Mama. He made you meatloaf for your birthday. We

should eat before it gets cold." Calli's voice cracked, and I could hear the raw emotion in it.

# Sixteen

## Calli

"I'm sorry about tonight," I said, leaning back on the porch swing next to Dylan.

I knew tonight would be hard with my mother, but I hadn't imagined how difficult it would be. Having Dylan there seemed to help keep her spirits up after I had to give in and tell her that my dad had died. I wanted to ignore it and move past it like the doctor had advised me to, but when her anxiety spurred into a full-blown panic attack that he wasn't there, I had no choice.

"Please don't apologize. There's nothing to be sorry about. If anything, I'm sorry that I couldn't do more."

He gently squeezed my hand, the warmth of it comforting despite the hot summer air.

"You did plenty. Thank you."

My mom decided to call it a night a little while ago, but I waited until I knew that she was okay before stepping outside with Dylan. He'd been a champ through it all and gave us the space we needed to get her situated. Never once did he complain, though he didn't seem like the kind of guy who ever complained about much, to begin with.

"If you could have any superpower in the world, what would it be and why?" He turned to face me, his face illuminated under the gentle beam of the porch light.

"Hmm. I don't know." I laughed a little and gave it some

serious thought. "What are my options?"

He leaned back and linked his fingers with mine before answering.

"Anything. Whatever your heart desires."

I tapped my finger to my chin, not missing the way his eyes followed my every movement.

"If I could have any superpower in the world, I would want the ability to read minds. Then I would know what people wanted without them having to tell me. Like my mom, I would be able to know what she was thinking, and maybe that would help me deal with her dementia better."

He smiled, but there was sadness lurking beneath it. I hated that I kept ruining the date by bringing everyone down. I shook my head, attempting to clear the dreary thoughts from it.

"Okay, your turn. What superpower would you want?"

"Easy," he said, not missing a beat. "I'd want to be invisible."

I raised my eyebrows and felt my lips curl up into a smile.

"Such a guy response," I teased. "Let me guess, that way you can spy on naked people?"

"Nope." He shook his head. "I want to be invisible so I can go around and do things for people without them knowing. Small acts of kindness that make their day better."

"Wow. I honestly wasn't expecting that," I admitted, pulling my head back.

"Don't get me wrong, I wouldn't mind checking out a hot naked girl, but I would never do that without her consent."

"You're such a nice guy." I leaned into him and bumped my shoulder against his.

"Thank you."

He turned to kiss my cheek at the same time I turned my head, our lips softly brushing against each other.

We both stilled for a moment, neither rushing to break the kiss.

My heart drummed in my chest, beating wildly out of control as the butterflies swarmed through me. My fingers itched to touch him, to feel the softness of his skin.

He started to pull back, and I could tell that he was going to apologize for it by the frown marring his forehead.

"I'm not sorry if you're not," I whispered, turning and sliding my hand behind his head before bringing my mouth to his again.

"I'm not at all," he muttered before my lips pressed against his.

I hadn't kissed a ton of guys in my life and had dated even fewer, but I didn't need a lot of experience to know that Dylan was a phenomenal kisser.

I leaned in closer, parting my lips as his tongue swiped across them. His hands wrapped around my waist as I climbed over and straddled him, not at all concerned that any of my nosey neighbors might be watching.

He deepened the kiss, his hands roaming down my waist to my ass.

I groaned into his mouth, my body slowly coming alive and wanting more from him.

My fingers scratched down his neck as my hips lifted, then lowered deeper over his groin.

"Calli," he panted, my name sounding beautiful on his lips.

"I want it too," I assured him, rocking back then forward to show him just how much.

"No, Calli. We have to stop."

His hands lifted from my ass, held out at his sides as if he was afraid to touch me.

"What happened? What's wrong?" I asked, not having the oxygen needed in my brain to process what had forced him to stop.

"We, um, have an audience."

He nodded behind me, so I turned my head and caught my mom's elderly neighbors watching us. The woman had a scowl on her face while her husband appeared to be amused.

"Hello, Sheriff Michaels. Evening, Sandra."

Dylan waved politely in their direction as I climbed off of his lap and adjusted my dress.

I heard a door slam shut and glanced over to find they had gone inside.

"Oh my God," I muttered, hiding my face behind my hands. "I can't believe that just happened. I'm so embarrassed. *That* was the *Sheriff*?"

"Yeah, but don't worry. He's pretty cool. I doubt we'll get arrested for it."

"Arrested!" My eyebrows shot up to my head. "What are you talking about?" I hissed, trying to keep my voice down so I didn't wake my mother.

"Well, this *is* a small town, and they don't take too well to people fornicating in public."

His eyes lit up as he said it.

"Stop it!" I laughed, smacking his arm playfully. "We weren't *fornicating*," I whispered the last word, too embarrassed to say it out loud.

"No, we weren't. But imagine if we had that invisibility

power. That might have come in handy just now." He winked and held his hand out to help me off the swing.

"I should get going since it's getting late and the gossip is going to start any minute now."

"You're kidding, right?" I scrunched my face.

"No, it's really late. Look around you. The sun went down hours ago."

I shook my head and laughed, thankful that Dylan could easily lighten my mood.

"Well, thank you for coming over tonight. Maybe one day we can have a real date where it doesn't include my mom and where we don't become the town's gossip."

"Thank you for the invite. Tonight was wonderful, and I look forward to the next time we get to hang out."

He leaned in and kissed my cheek, giving me a hug before pulling away and heading to his truck. And just like that, I didn't want the night with him to end.

# <u>Seventeen</u>

## Dylan

"Did you kiss her again? Like *kiss her*, kiss her?" Ramona asked, sitting cross-legged on the floor in front of the coffee table.

We gathered around Maggie's living room, eating Chinese take-out since our weekly plans were foiled again last night. It was becoming more common that we missed our Saturday night dinners, and I wondered how long they would keep going before they stopped completely. Before, it was easy because we were all single. Now, not so much.

"Kiss her. Kiss her. Kiss her fucker face," Pablo said, squawking from his cage in the corner, his gray feathers ruffled as he shook them.

"That's enough out of you," Ramona scolded. "You need to use nice words."

"Nice words. Nice words. Pecker head is a nice word."

Ramona rolled her eyes, then stuffed the last bite of eggroll into her mouth before returning her attention to me.

"So," she said around her food. "Did you kiss her again? Did more happen?"

I felt my skin heat as embarrassment washed over me as I thought about Calli straddling me on her front porch and trying to take things further.

"Maybe." I lifted the chopsticks to my mouth and took a bite.

"Maybe?" Maggie questioned as she adjusted on the couch, balancing her take-out container on a pillow. "What does that mean?"

"It means he totally did. Look at how red his face is." Ramona pointed in my direction, completely calling me out.

"Red face. Red face. Someone sits on your face." Pablo bounced around in his cage.

Ramona had someone drop Pablo off at her pet shop, Cool Cats, a while back. She had taken the African Gray parrot in and tried to teach it some manners, but it was completely hopeless. He had lived in a *colorful* house, to say the least. Now he lived with Maggie and Owen, as well as an underwear-stealing turtle, who had snuck up on me and was trying to steal my napkin.

"Nope, not today, Leroy," I said, gently pulling it away and redirecting him to the plate of lettuce he had down by his cage.

"Do you think he thinks it's underwear?" Ramona asked, all of us watching him scamper off.

"I think he hopes that's what it is. He hasn't touched his real food in days, but the vet said not to worry just yet. It might be the summer heat getting to him." Maggie's face fell as she stared at him. "Or maybe he's just missing Owen while he's at his work conference. I don't blame him; I haven't wanted to eat either."

"I bet you he would start eating again in no time if you gave him some of *Victoria's finest*." Ramona winked and then grabbed another eggroll from the bag.

"Victoria's finest?" I asked, completely confused as thoughts of Calli possibly wearing a thong the other night floated through my head.

"Yeah, from Victoria's Secret. He'll eat any panties he finds, but those are his favorite."

"I really didn't need to know that," I teased.

"So, how was it?" Maggie asked, tilting her head as she waited.

"How was what?" I took another bite and tried to get myself to stay focused on the conversation and not let my mind wander with thoughts of Calli.

"The kiss!" She threw her hands in the air, almost knocking over the container on her pillow.

I pretended that I had taken a big bite that I needed to chew to buy myself a few minutes.

"It was fine." I shrugged, feeling the heat of their gazes burning into me. It was weird being on the receiving end of this conversation and I wasn't willing to talk to them about the raging boner I constantly had for Calli.

"Fine? Just fine? Why does he always say that?" Ramona asked Maggie, completely ignoring me. "Whenever we ask him how things are going with Calli, he just says *fine* and acts like it's nothing." Finally, she turned to me and pointed a chopstick in my direction. "You're starting to piss me off."

Maggie's eyes widened though it wasn't really a surprise for either of us, given that we knew Ramona's love language was acts of violence.

"Okay, okay," I said, holding my hands in front of me to ward off the looks I was receiving. "It was more than fine. It was wonderful. Exceptional. The perfect kiss that I never want to end. And yes, it led to more, but we haven't acted on any of our urges yet."

"Awww," Maggie said softly, her eyes watering.

"There, that's better. Now we're getting somewhere," Ramona said, pleased with herself for getting an answer out of me that she liked. "When are you guys seeing each other again?"

I pushed my container to the side and leaned back against the recliner I was sitting in front of. I was too full to get up to throw my trash right away, and Leroy was on the other side of the room trying to eat the fake flowers painted on the side of one of Maggie's casserole dishes so I didn't have to worry about him.

"I don't know. We haven't made plans for another date yet."

"Why? Did something happen?"

"No," I said softly, picking at a loose thread on the bottom of my shirt. "We're just taking it slow. That's all."

The girls both made *aww* noises before Maggie shifted gears and asked how Cool Cats was doing with all of the new businesses popping up in that part of town. I let out a heavy sigh, thankful for Maggie saving me when she didn't even know how much I needed it.

Things were fine with Calli but I didn't want to talk about her and her mom with anyone without her being there. It felt too much like gossip, and that wasn't who I was when it came to people I really lov—shit. The realization that I was falling in love with Calli hit me hard and came from out of the blue.

# Eighteen
## Calli

"It has *what* in it?"

The older woman leaned in and tried to read the words on the menu board behind me, clearly not believing what I just said.

"It's a grilled cheese sandwich with a few slices of honey ham and mustard, then right before serving it, we add a layer of potato chips inside. It's served with a small side of chips and spicy maple bourbon pickle chips. It's that perfect combination of sweet and spicy with a satisfying crunch mixed in there."

"Okay," she sighed, slapping the counter as she smiled. "You sold me on it. I'll take one of the Poppin Grilled Cheese with water, please."

I grinned and rang her up before guiding her to the drink station to select her beverage, just in case she wanted something other than water.

It was busy for a Monday afternoon, but then again, it was busy all the time lately. We had a constant line out the door from the moment we opened until closing at 3:30. A handful of regulars had begged me to consider staying open through the evening since there wasn't a *decent* dinner place nearby.

I'd considered it, but until I could get the help I needed to keep Cravings afloat, it wasn't something I could do just yet. It would be amazing to reach that level of success so early on, but I would be lying if I said that I wasn't waiting for the other shoe to drop. It felt like things were going *too* well in my life right now, which was unnerving because I didn't know what was going to fall apart first. But history had shown that as soon as things felt like they were perfect, something always happened to mess that up.

I manned the register until Colby returned from his lunch and took over. I headed to the kitchen and checked on how everything was going, though there were no complaints up front, which should have proved everyone had a handle on things.

Paisley was at one of the back counters with my mom, laughing about something she had said. I smiled and walked over, grinning when I saw my mom making sandwiches. She had a loaf of bread out with a jar of peanut butter, a bottle of syrup, and a bag of chips she must have stolen from the guys when they weren't looking.

The grilled cheese was the most popular item today, and I knew we would have to stock up on more chips before we offered it again. But even though my mom had started out craving the grilled cheese sandwich this morning, her craving seemed to change by the time lunch came around.

"The key is to mix them together before spreading them on the bread," Mom said, guiding Paisley through the process for what was probably the millionth time in her life. But Paisley gave Mom her undivided attention and hung onto every word that came out of her mouth as if it were pure gold. Which, these days, we both did.

"Once you have the right consistency, you can start assembling your sandwich. Charlie always liked when I added an extra piece of bread so he could have a layer in between without it getting too soggy. Plus, I think he just liked having another spot to add more chips."

She nudged Paisley with her elbow, her eyes sparkling as she laughed.

Paisley caught my eye and held it, silently asking if I had noticed what my mom said.

It was the first time in—I couldn't remember how long, that my mom referred to my dad in the past. It was like she recalled that he had passed and was clearly present without the dementia taking over. These moments were so scarce that I didn't want to miss a single one.

"Hey guys, something smells good over here. What are you making?" I asked, pushing the emotion away so I could talk past the lump in my throat.

I stepped up to the counter and placed my hands on it to keep from nervously fidgeting.

"I'm making your favorite," my mom said, looking up at me with pride. "Peanut butter and syrup sandwiches with chips. Sit down and I'll make you one."

"Thanks, Mom." I pulled a metal stool over and sat down, glancing around the kitchen to make sure no one needed me. Lucas gave me a nod, letting me know he had everything under control so I could enjoy lunch with my mom.

Paisley grabbed the other two stools and set one to the side for my mom before taking a seat on hers. It felt like we were little girls again, eagerly awaiting lunch after spending hours playing outside in the sun and coming in famished.

Mom finished assembling the sandwiches and passed a plate to each of us before taking her seat and sitting down. She looked at the sandwich in front of her, a flurry of emotions swimming across her face, and worry began to fill me. Had the moment passed already? Had I already lost her to the fogginess of her disease again?

"What's wrong?" I asked softly, reaching my hand out and touching hers.

She looked up at me and shook her head.

"Nothing is wrong, dear. I just got lost in a memory. That's all."

She smiled, but it didn't reach her eyes. Without speaking another word, she lifted her sandwich and began eating. Paisley and I did the same, both too afraid to tarnish the moment.

************

By 3:15, my feet were aching, and I was ready for the day to be over. I was up front, sitting at one of the tables by the window when I heard the bell ding as the door opened. Dread rushed through me at the thought of another customer to serve when most of my staff had already gone home for the day. I tried to handle the end of day stuff by myself so I didn't stretch the team too thin when I really needed them during the peak busy hours.

I set the pen down and pushed away from the table, trying my best to put on a happy face even though I was too exhausted for it. Once I got to the register, I pulled my shoulders back and smiled.

"Welcome to Crav—." I shut my mouth and blinked a few times to ensure I wasn't hallucinating. "Dylan! What are you doing here?"

"Would you believe I'm here for a glass of water?" he asked, lifting his arm to wipe the sweat from his brow.

"I would, actually. It's hotter than a witch's tit out there."

"A what?" His cheeks showed off their deep dimples as he smiled, genuinely tickled by what I said.

"A witch's tit. It's something my grandma used to say." I waved my hand dismissively. "Let's just forget I said that. Did you want anything else besides the water?"

"Na, I'm good. Thank you. I didn't want to come bug you since it's so close to closing time, but I forgot my extra water bottle at home today, and the fountain outside is broken."

"You're never bugging me," I assured him. "Did you eat lunch?"

He shook his head.

"No time. We have to finish the rest of the strip mall by the end of September, and we're already a little behind."

"How many buildings do you have left?"

"Four if I can crank this last one out in the next few days."

"Dylan, it's like a hundred degrees out there. Spending that much time working in the sun without enough water and not eating can't be healthy. You're going to get sick."

"I'll be fine, I promise."

I glanced at my watch and then looked up at him.

"Can you give me five minutes?" I asked.

"Sure…." He eyed me suspiciously. "Does it take that long to get ice water?"

"No, smart ass. I'm going to make you lunch. Do you want something to drink besides water?"

"You don't have to do that, Calli."

"I know that I don't *have* to. I want to. Now sit down, take a break, and grab yourself some water. I'll make your lunch real quick."

"Thank you. I appreciate it."

Dylan grabbed the cup I handed him and went to the drink station, refilling his cup twice before I even had a chance to get started on his sandwich. I didn't want to cost him more time by cooking for him, but I also wanted him to take a break. It was sweltering outside, and I didn't want him to risk getting heat sick because he was so concerned with winning a bet.

I put together a grilled ham and cheese sandwich for him and looked through the fridge to see what fresh fruit I had left from breakfast this morning. I didn't want him to think he had to sit inside to eat it, so I packaged his sandwich with a side of chips, put the fruit in a separate to-go container, and bagged it all up. To make sure that he had everything he needed, I grabbed a few bottles of Gatorade out of the mini fridge I kept in my office and added them to his stuff.

When I went back up front, he was refilling his cup again, this time looking more refreshed with the redness in his face subsiding.

I held out the bag to him and smiled when he took it.

"It's nothing special. Grilled cheese and some fruit. Mainly watermelon and cantaloupe to help hydrate you."

"That was very considerate of you, thank you. How much is my total?" he asked, reaching for his wallet.

"It's my treat. Now get out there and finish that roof," I said playfully, loving the smile he was giving me.

He leaned in and pressed a light kiss to my lips. I walked him out and locked the door, officially closed for the day.

# Nineteen

## Dylan

My head hurt almost as bad as my body from working a double shift today. I wasn't sure if you could even technically call it that, but given that my day started at three this morning and didn't end until after seven, it felt like it should be.

I got home and fought the urge to pass out on the couch. I wanted nothing more than to sleep for seven days solid, but I was sweaty and sticky and needed a shower first. After cleaning up, I warmed a slice of leftover pizza and shoved it down my throat. More the process of eating because I had to than eating because I wanted to. I finally gave in around eight and crawled into bed, ready for sleep.

Just as my eyes fluttered shut, I heard my phone ding.

Normally, I would ignore it and let it go until tomorrow when I was hopefully well-rested and wanted to deal with whoever it was. But the thought that it could be Calli had me reaching for it within seconds.

A smile spread across my face as I saw her name.

**Calli: Hey, just checking in to see how you're feeling. I'm sure you're used to working like this in the extreme heat, but I've been worried about you.**

My fingers flew quickly across the screen, eager to talk to her.

**Me: I'm fine, thank you for checking. I just cooled off in a quick shower and ate some leftover pizza.**

Me: How are you? How was your day?

Calli: It was good. Busy. But I had a nice lunch with my mom. That was nice.

Me: How is she doing?

Calli: Today was a good day. She seemed more like herself and didn't struggle to remember things as much as she has been lately. It was weird, but I have never been more thankful to have my mom back.

Calli: I feel bad for saying that. I have my mom, but it just feels like she slips further and further away as this disease progresses.

Me: That's a valid feeling. You shouldn't feel bad about that. I can't imagine how hard this has been on both of you.

Calli: Sorry, I didn't mean to turn this into a sad text.

Me: You didn't. (Smiley emoji)

Calli: Yes, I did. It's okay; I can fix this. Let me think of something funny…

Me: Like the temperature of a witch's tit?

Calli: You're not going to let me live that one down, are you?

Me: I think the real question is how you know how hot a witch's tit is. Or better yet, how your grandma knew.

Calli: I'm trying so hard not to laugh right now. You're gonna make me wake my mom up.

Me: Hey, you started it.

Calli: It's better than the sad conversation.

Me: Any conversation with you is a good conversation. Good or bad—I'll take all of it.

**Calli: Thank you. I enjoy talking to you too. Though it's getting late, and I have a feeling I'm keeping you up.**

**Me: It's worth it.**

**Calli: No, it's not. You need sleep.**

**Me: Says who?**

**Calli: Me.**

**Me: So bossy…**

**Calli: I have only the best intentions. The last thing I want is for you to fall off a roof because you were sleep deprived because of me.**

**Me: Again, it would be worth it.**

**Calli: I need to call it a night too. I've got an early morning tomorrow and slept like shit last night. Come see me in the morning, and I'll make you some coffee.**

**Me: What time will you be there?**

**Calli: Five.**

**Me: Cool. I'll see you in the morning.**

**Calli: Goodnight. Sleep well.**

**Me: You too. Sweet dreams.**

I waited to see if another text message was going to come through, but she just hearted the message I sent and that was it. I put my phone back on the wireless charger and crashed out.

# <u>Twenty</u>

## Calli

It was funny how my body knew that Dylan was close by before I did. I felt goosebumps pebble across my skin as he pulled the door open, and the bell chimed above. I pulled my shoulders back, thankful I had taken the extra time this morning to get ready before he came in. I told him I would be here by five, but I hadn't been able to sleep last night and showed up at four-thirty instead.

"Good morning," he said, looking amazing even though I could tell he was still tired.

"Good morning," I replied, the stress in my body melting away as his fingers brushed mine when he took the to-go cup I offered him. "I made the same as last time, and there's a tray ready for you to take up to the guys."

"You're spoiling them, you know."

"Eh, it's just coffee. I wouldn't call that spoiling."

"Trust me—it's better than anything we make at home. It's definitely spoiling us but don't tell Maggie that I said that."

"Your secret is safe with me." I pretended to zip my lips. "Though I could totally go for a honey lavender latte from Spill The Beans this morning."

I grabbed one the other day while running errands during lunch and quickly became obsessed.

"Want me to bring you one later?" he offered, taking a sip.

I shook my head quickly.

"Oh no, that's okay. Thank you, I appreciate the offer, but you don't need to take time out of your day to bring me coffee."

I knew how busy he was this week with trying to finish the strip mall, so the last thing I wanted him to do was to fall behind because he did something nice and brought me a latte that I didn't need.

"The offer is always there." He winked and tapped his knuckles on the counter before grabbing the tray. "Thank you again for this."

I heard the bell chime as he left, leaving me alone with my thoughts of him and how I had never met anyone as nice and selfless as Dylan. I sucked in a slow, deep breath and tried to clear the fuzzy feelings he left inside me. When I looked down, I spotted a fifty-dollar bill where the tray had been and shook my head.

That little stinker.

I popped it into the cash register, then downed the rest of my coffee and got the day started before I had the chance to fall behind again.

By nine, I got a text message from Paisley that my mom wasn't feeling well. She had swung by to pick her up to bring her to Cravings with her since I came in so early. She asked if I wanted her to come to work or to stay with my mom. I immediately asked her to stay with Mom and to call me if anything happened.

Not having Paisley there meant we were busier than usual since we were shorthanded. I was running the kitchen as well as taking out orders, just to keep our heads above water. Since my mom wasn't there today, I didn't have her cravings to go off of, so I kept the menu simple. It was supposed to be another hot day with record-breaking temperatures, so I played on that and had a variety of spicy foods paired with some fun chilled salad options for those who didn't want anything hot.

I had spent the morning doing the prep work for the salads while Lucas worked on the sauce for the wings. We also had the spicy tuna wrap that everyone loved, which made it convenient that we didn't have to do a lot of explaining today about what each food was and what was in it.

Things were bustling in the kitchen when one of the kids that was helping out up front came back to get me.

"What's up?" I asked, barely looking up as I finished putting the cobb salad together.

"Someone is asking for you."

"Do you know who it is?" I lifted my head slightly, making eye contact with the overly angsty teenager who was way too emo and moody to work at Cravings. I was thankful for the help, but I could only imagine what people thought when they encountered him.

"Yeah."

I sliced the egg and added it to the top of the salad before pushing it to the side to finish the tuna wrap that went with the order.

"Okay," I said with an edge to my tone. "Who is it?"

The kid opened his mouth to say something but was interrupted.

"It's me," Dylan said, walking into the kitchen. "Sorry, I realized it was probably easier to come back here and tell you myself."

He gave me a sympathetic smile as the kid shrugged his shoulder, tossed his long bangs out of his eyes, and went back up front.

"Please tell me you have Kody clearing the tables and not

helping customers?" he asked teasingly.

"That's what he's supposed to be doing. Colby should be at the register," I replied, standing on my tiptoes to confirm.

"Don't worry, he is. I was just teasing you. I know how *personable* Kody can be."

"You're telling me," I laughed as I placed the tuna wrap on the paper and rolled it up. "Kate, can you please run this order up for me?"

I wiped my hands on my apron and took a moment to catch my breath.

"You guys are super busy today," Dylan noted, handing me a to-go cup from Spill The Beans. "I thought you could use an afternoon pick me up."

My heart thumped wildly in my chest, touched by his thoughtfulness.

"Thank you, that was very sweet of you. I definitely need a pick-me-up. Paisley is out today, so we're short-staffed. My mom wasn't feeling well this morning, so she stayed with her to keep an eye on her."

Dylan's eyebrows pulled together.

"Oh no, I'm sorry to hear that. Do they need anything? I can make a quick run to the store and drop it off."

"They're good, but thank you. Paisley said that Mom has been sleeping most of the day. She seems run down and tired, nothing a little rest can't cure."

He nodded and shoved his hands into his pockets.

"I didn't get a chance to ask this morning, but were you able to get some rest last night?" I asked, taking a long sip of the latte. I closed my eyes and allowed myself to drift off to heaven for just a few seconds. Whatever Maggie put in here was pure magic.

"I did. I could've slept a few more hours, but I'm good."

I smiled and tried to ignore the calls flying through the kitchen as more orders came in. I wanted to talk to Dylan and spend time with him, but we were already sinking again with just the few minutes I had stopped to thank him for the coffee.

"I'll let you go," he said quickly, completely aware of how tense I was getting by the second. "I did want to ask if you have plans Friday night."

"Nope, none that I know of. Why?"

"Our guys got ahead of schedule, which means the new movie theater is opening. I thought maybe I could take you to a movie if you were up for it."

"I would love that."

"Cool. I'll text you later, and we can figure out the plans. Have a good day, Calli."

I could tell he wanted to lean in and kiss me as much as I wanted him to. But we had a kitchen full of people waiting for me to dive in and help get the madness under control, so I gave a small wave and got back to work.

# Twenty-One

## Dylan

"Can we get a large popcorn with extra butter, two large drinks, a box of peanut M&M's, and a box of Reese's Pieces?" I slid my card across the counter to the kid ringing up our treats for the movie tonight.

It was busy for opening night, just like I had assumed it would be. It was the first movie theater to open in Whiskey Mountain, so the locals were ecstatic about it. When I went online to grab tickets for Calli and me, almost everything was already sold out.

I lucked out and got two seats for some action-packed movie I had seen previews for. I wasn't sure whether Calli would enjoy it, but she assured me she liked anything and wasn't picky. I grabbed the big bucket of popcorn while Calli tucked the candy boxes into her purse and then grabbed the cups to fill them.

"What would you like?" she asked, standing in front of the soda dispenser.

"Root beer, please."

"You got it." She smiled and began filling the cup with ice before moving it over to fill hers. I watched her work, partly feeling bad that I couldn't easily help her with my hands full, but also thankful for the opportunity to take in her beauty.

*She was breathtakingly gorgeous.*

Once we had our drinks, we made our way to our seats. Unfortunately, when I got our tickets, the only seats that were left were in the very back, in the corner. I didn't want Calli to think that I had done that on purpose to try to take advantage of her in a dark theater, but it was either those seats or none at all.

"Sorry," I apologized as we sat down. "These were the only seats they had."

"They're perfect," she assured me, setting my drink in the cup holder.

I wasn't sure what to expect with the new theater, given that we were in a small town, but I was pleasantly surprised to find that each seat was plenty roomy and reclined. The amount of space we had between seats made me feel better that this wasn't an accidental step toward *creeper* status.

I wanted to say more and tell her how beautiful she looked tonight, but before I could, the lights dimmed, and the previews started playing on the big screen in front of us. I leaned back in my chair and handed her the bucket of popcorn, not trusting myself not to knock it over.

My phone buzzed in my pocket, so I quickly pulled it out and tried to hide it so I didn't disrupt anyone with the screen's brightness compared to the theater's darkness. There was a new text message from Maggie in the group thread with me, her, and Ramona.

**Maggie: Have fun on your date tonight! Can't wait to hear all about it!**

I grinned and texted back before shoving my phone back into my pocket. I felt it vibrate again but ignored it, knowing that either Maggie had hearted my *thank you* reply or Ramona had said something. I was there to spend time with Calli, so I wanted to make sure my attention was where it needed to be and not stuck on my phone.

"Everything okay?" Calli whispered, leaning in close

enough that I could smell the light scent of her perfume.

Her hair was piled loosely on her head, with a few wispy curls tucked behind her ear.

"Everything is perfect." I lifted her hand and kissed it.

She grinned and turned back to the movie, not bothering to pull her hand away until the movie started and she needed it to fish out the candy from her purse. She handed me the box of Reese's Pieces and then opened her box of peanut M&M's, offering me one.

"Try them with the popcorn. It's the perfect combination," she gushed, her face lit up like a kid on Christmas morning.

I took a few and popped them into my mouth, then added a few pieces of popcorn. I chewed and closed my eyes, savoring the taste.

"That's delicious." I smiled at her and then offered her some of my candy. She took a few, popped them into her mouth, and added some popcorn. Her eyes widened in delight.

"I'm not sure which I like better," she admitted quietly.

"Help yourself to them whenever you want."

She smiled again and I felt it deep inside my heart.

I turned my attention to the movie so I wouldn't sit there and fixate on Calli, though it was hard not to when her arm would gently brush against mine. I took some deep breaths and tried to pay attention to the action happening on the screen instead of thinking about the action that could be happening between Calli and me every time her leg pushed a little closer to mine, making her sundress ride up higher.

# Twenty-Two

## Calli

"Thank you for the movie tonight," I said, pressing my hands together in front of me as we walked to his truck.

"Thank you for coming."

My eyes widened at the hidden innuendo he hadn't meant to put down, though I was quick to snatch it up. I couldn't stop thinking about Dylan lately, and the constant way my body buzzed every time he was around me had me taking everything he said the wrong way. Wishful thinking, such wishful thinking…

He cleared his throat and looked up at the night sky before looking back at me.

"I really enjoyed your company tonight, Calli."

I giggled, loving the moments when he would get so flustered around me. I liked to think that maybe it was because of me, but I didn't want to get my hopes up only to be let down if he wasn't exactly on the same page as me. It *felt* like he was, but I had been wrong before.

"I enjoyed yours too," I replied, taking his hand as he helped me into the truck.

I sat down and smoothed down the bottom of my dress as he climbed into the driver's seat and started the engine. I was disappointed that the movie was already over because I didn't want my time with Dylan to end. As if the universe could sense my unease, my phone vibrated in my purse.

I pulled it out and found a text message from Paisley, letting me know my mom had gone to bed and that she would stay there until I got back. She was starting a Harry Potter marathon which meant she would be staying the night and continuing any movies she didn't finish tonight tomorrow. Likely combined with mimosas and brunch that I would be lured into making.

"Everything alright?" Dylan asked, looking over at me before returning his focus to the road.

"Yeah, Paisley is staying at my house tonight, so she was just letting me know that my mom was already in bed, so I don't have to rush home."

I felt the heat rise through my veins as I thought about having a free night with Dylan without worrying about getting home. He hadn't asked me to stick around, yet he seemed to be driving slower than usual, delaying taking the street to my house.

"Oh. That's good. Is she feeling better?"

"She's been a little tired still, but overall doing good. Paisley has been great with helping out when I need her to. I didn't even have to ask her to stay over tonight; she just volunteered." I laughed nervously.

He shifted in his seat, seeming a tad bit uncomfortable.

"So, umm. Did you want to keep hanging out? I can take you home if you'd rathe—."

"I would love to," I interrupted, cutting him off before he could finish his sentence.

His cheeks split into the goofy grin I loved as his grip on the steering wheel relaxed a little.

"Was there anything you wanted to do?" he asked.

I shook my head, hoping he didn't catch the blush covering

my face, giving away exactly what I wanted to do.

He chewed his lip while he looked around.

"I don't think much will be open this late. But we can go back to my place if you want to. I have more board games," he offered.

"Sounds perfect."

I leaned back in the seat and took a few steading breaths as I tried to remind myself that this wasn't my first time, nor was there even a guarantee that we were going to have sex tonight.

Once we got to his house, he parked and then came around to help me out. I loved the way his hands held onto me, gentle yet strong. It was nice having unexpected free time with him, and I didn't want to waste a single second of it, knowing that it might be hard to come by this opportunity again anytime soon.

He held my hand as I stepped down, his other hand sliding down to my lower back. I turned to face him, not realizing he had stepped closer, and smacked into his chest.

"Sorry," I murmured, not wanting to look up as my body pressed tightly against his.

"Don't be."

Without second-guessing anything or giving myself a chance to back out, I reached up, wrapped my hands around his neck, and brought my lips to his.

I thought the kiss would be soft and romantic, but his mouth swiped over mine hungrily, capturing the moan that floated through my lips. His hands slipped down my ass, lifting me to his hips as my legs locked around him.

We continued kissing, not bothering to care if anyone was watching, as he walked us to the door, unlocked it, and promptly kicked it shut with his foot. Nothing could stop us now as we made out, our hands grabbing whatever we could as we frantically tried to rip each other's clothes off.

"Are you sure?" he asked as my fingers desperately tried to work the button on his jeans.

"Yes," I breathed, finally getting it undone and pulling down the zipper. "I've wanted this for weeks, Dylan."

"Me too."

He gently pulled me off his body and set me on my feet while I tried to catch my breath. He grabbed the back of his shirt with one hand and pulled it over his ridiculously sculpted body. He was gorgeous. Absolutely perfect.

I licked my lips, ready to worship his body if he would just strip off the last of his clothes so I could.

"No. Me first," he said as if reading my mind.

I nodded, my brain struggling to process what was happening as all the blood rushed to my pelvis. He watched me with lust-filled eyes and kissed me gently while lifting my dress over my body and tossing it to the floor.

Thankfully I had planned ahead, *hoping* that this might happen, and had worn the new black lace lingerie I'd bought earlier this week. I knew things could happen between us at any time, given the constant combustible energy that flowed between us, and I was thankful that tonight was going to be the night.

He stepped back and looked me up and down, soaking up every detail as his eyes took their time going the length of my body. I didn't miss how his Adam's apple bulged as he tried to swallow when he landed on the thin patch of lace that was covering my sex. Wetness started to pool between my legs as I anxiously waited for his touch.

"You're so fucking beautiful," he whispered, dropping to his knees before me.

I was still standing there, wearing nothing but a bra and

thong panties, as he leaned in and placed a kiss on my stomach while his hands leisurely roamed my body. His touch was feather-light, leaving goosebumps in their wake, but it kept me craving more.

He tilted his head, his tongue dancing across my skin as he pulled my panties down and slid them down to the floor. My pussy was lined up right in front of his face, and when he looked up at me with a wicked smile, I almost lost it.

"Dylan," I pleaded, closing my eyes while I tried to keep my composure.

"I've got you, baby. Don't worry."

Without saying another word, he leaned in and pressed his face between my legs. Normally I would have been mortified to have someone see me naked with the lights on, let alone plant their head in my private parts. But with Dylan, it was different. He made me feel calm and relaxed, but not only that. He also made me feel sexy with the way he was worshiping my body right now.

His tongue was warm and wet as he licked my lips, slipping it in between before pulling back and sucking my clit. I spread my legs wider, allowing him more room. I still had my heels on, which made me feel a little naughty, even if I was worried that I might break an ankle wearing them in this position if I came. As if reading my thoughts again, Dylan sucked harder, sending a jolt right through me that served as a silent promise that he was going to get me there.

I grabbed the back of his head and held on, pushing it harder against me as he drove me closer to the edge.

"Dylan," I panted, desperate to grind myself against him.

"I know, baby."

He pulled away, and the disappointment rushed over me in waves.

"Sit on my face," he instructed as he laid down on the living room carpet and extended his hand to help me.

"I—"

"Sit. On. My. Face."

"But—"

"Damn it, Calli. Get your sexy ass down here now and sit on my face so I can finish eating your pussy. I know you're not going to let yourself come standing up, so you're going to ride my face until you do."

I wanted to say more and continue to object, but the way he looked at me had me taking his hand and climbing down on top of him.

I did my best to get into a squatting position to hold my weight and not smother him, but he quickly squashed that idea by grabbing my ass and keeping me in place so I couldn't move.

Within seconds, his tongue had found my clit again and flicked it mercilessly as my back arched.

"Ride my face," he muttered from beneath me.

Knowing that I wasn't going to get out of it, I did as he asked. I took a deep breath and spread my legs before planting my hand on the side of his head. I rocked my hips back and forth, creating the friction I needed from him.

I felt the tingling in my spine and knew that I was close.

He sucked harder, continuing to grip me firmly against his face as I rode it to climax.

"Ahhh," I cried out, my eyes closed as my muscles clenched and spasmed. "Fuck!"

He continued his delicious torture until my body stilled

around him and went limp. He placed his arms around my back and rolled me over, laying beside me so he could look into my eyes.

I tried not to freak out about the evidence of my arousal that was still streaked across his upper lip. While keeping his eyes locked on mine, he parted his lips and let his tongue slowly lick it off.

"If you were on the menu at Cravings, I would come in and eat you every day."

I arched an eyebrow while I tried not to laugh.

"Well, if I were on the menu, that would mean other people would too."

"Like fuck they would," he growled, pulling me closer to him. "I know we haven't talked about relationships and all that since we're taking this slow. But I can promise you one thing, Calli."

"What's that?"

"If I lick it, it's mine."

I covered my mouth and giggled.

"Oh really?"

"You bet your ass. Which I wouldn't mind licking either," he teased, his hand reaching down to grab it.

"Well, if the rule is that something is ours once we lick it, then your dick is about to be the property of Calli in just a few seconds."

His eyes darkened as I pushed him onto his back and began working his jeans off him. I stripped off his boxer briefs, not wasting any time getting what I wanted.

Once he was laid bare in front of me, I took a moment to take in the sight of him. How glorious his body was and how every single inch of him was ripped and defined by hours of hard work.

I grabbed his shaft and licked my lips, too eager to suck his cock to bother with starting slow. I brought him to my mouth and opened it, relaxing my jaw the best I could to accommodate his large size. He cursed under his breath as he reached the back of my throat and I felt his thighs tighten around me.

Dylan was beyond well-endowed, and I wanted nothing more than to have my fill of him—literally. I wanted to spend the entire night sucking his cock and then having him fuck me senseless because even though I had been with other guys before, none of them compared to Dylan.

I continued to work him in my mouth, pulling my head back before sucking him back down. My hands worked the rest of his shaft that didn't fit, teasing his balls as he got closer to coming. I wanted sex with Dylan to happen tonight, but I also wanted him to give in to his pleasure and come down my throat. How satisfying would it be to have a man lose control so quickly because of something I had done?

"I'm gonna come," he warned, trying to pull away from my mouth. Just like he'd done earlier, I gripped his hips and held him in place as I sucked faster and harder, taking him in and out of my mouth at the speed he liked until I felt the warm, salty ropes of cum shoot down the back of my throat.

I greedily sucked up every last drop, making sure I got it all before I slowly released his cock from my mouth. I chewed my lower lip as I laid down beside him and rested my head on his chest.

"You fucking own me, Calli. Whatever you want, it's yours." He closed his eyes as we lay there naked on the floor.

"Well, I kinda wanted your cock inside of me…" I teased playfully.

"Give me ten minutes to recover, and then I'll make that wish come true for you, baby."

I grinned and curled deeper into his side.

# Twenty-Three

## Dylan

"The pizza will be here in twenty minutes," I said, handing another bottle of water to Calli, who looked perfect sitting on my bed wearing nothing but one of my t-shirts.

"You didn't have to order food, but thank you."

"Like hell I didn't," I laughed. "I plan on fucking you senseless tonight and need the fuel to keep going."

"Two rounds weren't enough?" She giggled, and I loved the sound almost as much as I loved being with her. Being in her. Fuck, I just loved her.

"Not nearly. I hate to break it to you, baby, but I'm never going to get enough of you. Even while I'm fucking you, I'm going to be thinking about the next time I get to fuck you."

She shook her head and tried to hide her face behind a throw pillow.

I climbed on the bed and grabbed it from her, tossing it to the floor as I captured her lips with mine.

"Like right now, I already want you again," I said, pressing her hand to my crotch. After the second time being inside her, I stopped bothering to get dressed and just threw on a pair of sweatpants. They were easy enough to get off for moments like this when we knew we couldn't resist doing it again.

"This time, I want to be on top," she said quietly, chewing her lip again. They were already swollen from all the kissing we'd been doing, but the added nervous lip chewing kept them constantly puffy.

"Fuck yeah," I growled, grabbing another condom from the pile on top of the nightstand. Within seconds, I had my sweats off and sheathed myself before Calli climbed on and lowered herself onto my cock.

I hissed out a breath, so thankful that she seemed to be constantly wet around me. Even after cleaning her up each time, she was still so easily aroused by me that I felt a different connection with her. It was almost like it was a sign from the universe that we were meant to be together—we were a perfect fit, both figuratively and literally.

She didn't bother trying to keep her weight off of me—which I was happy about—as she ground her hips against me, rubbing her clit against my cock as she rode me. I could already tell she was getting close by the way she was tightening around me, and I wanted her to come again. I'd lost track of how many orgasms she'd had, but I knew it wasn't enough. It would never be enough.

"Use your fingers, baby. Rub your clit as you ride me. I want to see you touch yourself."

She nodded, locking eyes with me as she did as I asked. Her back was slightly arched, her nipples puckered through the thin fabric of the t-shirt.

"Wait," I said breathlessly. "Take your shirt off so I can see your perfect tits."

She grinned and pulled it over her head before tossing it to the floor.

I lifted my hips, meeting her thrust for thrust, wanting to be deeper inside her. She moaned as she used one hand to play with herself and the other to roll a tightened nipple between her fingers.

Right as she was on the cusp of coming, I heard the doorbell ring.

Fuck! On occasion, the pizza deliveries were quicker than they estimated, but tonight was the worst night for them to be ahead of schedule.

"Don't stop," I warned, grabbing my phone from the nightstand beside me. "Keep rubbing yourself until I tell you to stop."

She nodded and watched as I handled my phone.

"You can leave it there," I said, talking into the phone loud enough that the delivery person could hear it from the camera outside.

"Did you want any parmesan cheese or red pepper flakes?" the kid asked, looking up at the camera.

"No, thank you, we're good," I said, struggling to keep my composure as Calli rode me harder and faster. She had stopped rubbing herself with her finger, but I couldn't get mad when she was using my cock to get off.

"Okay." He turned to leave and then stopped and bent down to check the bag. "Sorry, I forgot the breadsticks in the car. Let me go grab them real quick."

I didn't bother to say anything as I closed my eyes and enjoyed Calli's soft moans. She dug her fingers into the sheets beside me, and her mouth parted.

The kid returned and set the other bag on top of the pizza box.

"Are you sure you don't want some cheese?" he asked, lifting his cap to scratch his head.

"Yes!" Calli screamed as she came hard and fast on my cock, her pussy clenching me so tightly that I struggled to hold off on mine while still watching the teenager on the camera app on my phone.

He nodded, grabbed a few from the outside pouch of the delivery bag, and set them on top of the breadsticks.

"Yes!" Calli screamed again.

He looked up and shrugged before adding another handful to the pile.

"Yes! Yes! Yes!" Her head tipped back as she finished spasming around me, but I couldn't take my eyes off my phone as I watched the kid dump the rest of the packets from his bag, shaking it vigorously to make sure they all came out.

"That's all I've got," he said, then turned and walked away.

I hadn't realized I had been holding the *talk* button the entire time. Thankfully I had already tipped him online, so I didn't have to face him after knowing that he heard Calli coming and thought her screams of ecstasy translated into a need for parmesan cheese packets.

"Oh my God," Calli sighed, rolling off of me slowly while I gripped the condom to make sure it didn't come off. "That was so intense."

I nodded, a cheeky grin consuming my face.

"It was fucking incredible."

"Did he hear me?" she asked cautiously, pulling the sheet over her.

"I'm pretty sure he did, given he brought a few pounds of parmesan cheese for us."

She covered her face and kicked her legs under the cover.

"Oh no! I'm going to get a reputation for being *that girl* in this town, aren't I?"

I grabbed the sheet and pulled it down despite her deathly cling to it.

"You're not *that girl*. You're *my* girl, and I don't care if people hear me fucking your brains out as long as I'm making you feel good. Now throw on a shirt so we can eat because I'm starving and if you dare try to eat pizza in front of me naked, I'm going to end up fucking you again *while* I eat it. Shit, I might even cover you in parmesan cheese, given that we have plenty."

I got up, pulled on my sweats, and winked at her before going out to collect our food.

# Twenty-Four

## Calli

"You seem distracted today," Paisley said as she wiped down the counter next to me. It was the first break we'd had at Cravings today and the first I had a chance to talk freely with her about what happened Friday night with Dylan. She'd stayed at my house that night, so she knew that *something* had happened when I didn't get home until six in the morning when she was already up and making coffee.

We'd spent Saturday on the couch continuing her Harry Potter marathon while my mom rested and tried to get into the movies. I knew Paisley had chosen them because they were Mom's favorite, but it was sad when she didn't know what they were and couldn't remember watching them before. Mom's knowledge of Harry Potter used to be so good that she could enter trivia contests and win.

Paisley and I had kept our conversations around safe topics that day, not venturing into anything that could upset Mom. Unfortunately, it left very little for us to talk about without excluding her, so we gave up and just spent the day watching other movies that Mom might enjoy once the marathon was over.

Yesterday I spent the day with Mom trying to do some light gardening, anything to get that light back in her eyes. I'd missed seeing it and it felt like it was diminishing more every day. By the time I made dinner, she was already tired and went to bed without eating. Her doctor assured me that she was okay and not to force her into doing things if she didn't need to.

I hadn't slept well last night after Dylan and I stayed up late sending dirty text messages about what we wanted to do to each other the next time we were together. After that, I was wound tight and overly sexually frustrated but unable to do anything about it. He had offered to call so we could have phone sex, but Mom had been just as restless as me, so I didn't want to risk her hearing anything.

"I'm just tired," I said dismissively with a shrug.

"Everything okay with you and Dylan?" she asked quietly, making sure no one else could hear our conversation. Most of the staff was in the kitchen, getting food prepped for the lunch rush, while a few were sitting at the tables in the front, wrapping silverware in napkins.

"Yeah, things are going good."

"But?" She turned and studied my face as if that would tell her the answer she was looking for.

"I don't know," I sighed, taking a seat on the stool behind me.

"Are you not feeling it with him anymore?" she pressed, hopping up onto the counter she had just cleaned.

"You're gonna have to wipe that down again," I said, pointing to where her butt was almost hanging out of her cutoff shorts on the counter.

She looked down and then wiggled some, making sure to spread her cheeks all over it.

"Everyone loves a little bit of ass," she teased with a wink.

Color filled my cheeks so quickly that I didn't have time to stop it.

Her eyebrows rose drastically high on her forehead.

"Did Dylan eat your ass?" she whispered loudly.

"Oh my God!" I screeched, swatting her leg. "PAISLEY!"

"What? I'm just saying that I wouldn't be complaining if someone ate my ass."

One of the guys from the back walked out right as she said it, then stopped, shook his head, and turned back to the kitchen. He was older and happily married to the love of his life, so I didn't expect him to linger around to hear whatever else came out of Paisley's mouth.

I arched an eyebrow in warning to her.

"Sorry." She shrugged. "Just saying that if Maverick busted through those doors asking if an ass sandwich was on the menu today, I would be the first to write it on the board so he could get what he wants."

I pressed a palm to my forehead and shook my head.

"What am I going to do with you?" I asked playfully.

"Tell me that you love me and thank me for packing up and moving down here with you—which you've already done."

"You know how grateful I am for everything you've done for me, Paisley. I couldn't do any of this without your help and support. And yes, I love you. You know that," I laughed.

"That I do. But I also know that something is going on with you and you're not telling me."

"There's nothing to tell."

"Bullshit."

I sighed heavily and folded my arms over my chest as I leaned back to rest my back against the wall. Thankfully the stool was old and didn't have wheels, so I didn't have to worry about shooting myself across the room.

"What's going on?" she pressed. "I know I tease and give you a lot of shit, but I also know you better than anyone, and I can tell that you're about to get in your head, which means you're going to get in your own way of happiness."

"You don't know that," I scoffed.

"Yes, I do. And if I had to bet money on it, I would say that something happened between you and Dylan—besides sex, duh. And whatever it is has you questioning whether or not you want to allow yourself to be in a relationship with him."

I opened my mouth to speak but snapped it shut when I realized she was right.

"It's complicated."

"Let's make it uncomplicated."

"It's not that easy," I muttered, desperate for the conversation to stop when I saw Dylan outside, heading in. "Can we please not talk about this right now?"

"Fine," she said, but then her tone changed from frustrated to flirty when she spotted Maverick walking in beside Dylan.

She hopped off the counter and tucked a strand of dark hair behind her ear before turning around and giving them her flirtiest smile.

"Hi, welcome to Cravings. What can we get you?"

I looked at her in disbelief, wondering if she was trying to sound like someone who worked at my restaurant or if she should pursue a career as a phone sex operator.

Maverick leaned against the wall, casually scanning the menu board behind us as Dylan headed straight for me.

"Hey," I said, standing up and leaning over the counter to hug him.

"Hey, beautiful."

I was thankful that even though we had spent hours together

naked and licking every inch of each other's body that he didn't try to kiss me. We hadn't gotten around to talking about what this thing was between us, even though it felt like we'd both agreed that we were seeing each other. We also hadn't discussed whether this was exclusive, but the way he growled *mine* every time he got near my pussy told me that I probably didn't need to worry about that. We'd licked each other's privates, so obviously, we'd called dibs on them, and that was the rule. But I wasn't quite ready to show off my new relationship with him at work.

"How are you?" he asked, giving me space as Paisley flirted shamelessly with Maverick at the other end of the counter.

"I'm good. A little tired," I admitted, my cheeks flushed with color when I thought about our text messages from last night.

"I'm sorry. I wish I could have been there to take care of that for you." He kept his voice low so only I could hear.

"I wish you could have too."

"Maybe we can hang out again this weekend?" he offered, his voice still low as he glanced over at Paisley and Maverick. "It doesn't have to be all night like last weekend, but I also won't say no if you're available and want to stay over again."

I shook my head, hating the feeling that was bubbling up inside of me.

"I don't think I can. My mom hasn't been having the best days lately, and I think I need to be around more often for her."

He nodded but I could see the disappointment etched on his face.

"I'm sorry—"

"Don't you dare apologize to me, Calli," he said softly, reaching over and squeezing my hand. "I will *never* ask you to put me before your mother, and I know how important it is for you to be there for her. We have all the time in the world, so please don't feel like there's a rush to find time for me."

I pulled my lips in and tried to stop the quivering that wanted to take over. I tried to smile, but it fell short and never reached my lips.

"Hey, Calli, do you know where we would have some extra parmesan packets? I can't seem to find them anywhere," Paisley asked as she ducked beneath the counter to where the extra supplies were kept. "I swear, it's like everyone is out. Some kind of shortage or something."

I had just taken a sip of my iced coffee when she asked and sputtered it across the counter as I thought about what Dylan and I did with all of the cheese packets we had the other night. Paisley's head popped up and she gave me a weird look as I quickly grabbed some napkins and cleaned up my mess.

"They're in a box in the back," I answered.

Dylan smirked, licking his lips as he watched my flustered reaction. I took a deep breath and tried to remind myself that I was a businesswoman who needed to get her shit together and quit acting like a horny teenager.

# Twenty-Five

## Dylan

I missed Calli all week and the only thing that got me through not seeing her this weekend was the sexy picture she sent me a few hours ago. It wasn't a nude one—though I wouldn't have complained if it was. But Calli wasn't that kind of girl, and that's what I loved about her.

Instead, it was a selfie she'd taken in the kitchen while making dinner for her mom. Patti had been having a harder time this week, so Calli wanted to spend time with her one-on-one. They were having chicken pot pie with mashed potatoes for dinner, and Calli made the dough from scratch.

I tried to keep my attention focused on Maggie and Ramona while at dinner tonight but cut it short when they wanted to stay at La Salsa and have a few drinks. It was Saturday night, and I finally had a night to hang out with my friends where no one had to rush off to something else. But instead of hanging out, I faked having a headache, paid the bill, and got out of there so I wouldn't feel bad staring at my phone all night while waiting to hear from Calli.

As soon as I got home, I kicked off my shoes and headed to my room to change when I heard it ding with a new text message. I pulled it out of my pocket and grinned when I saw Calli's name.

**Calli: How was dinner tonight?**

**Me: It was good. How was dinner with your mom?**

**Calli: It was fine. She wasn't up for much, so she ate and**

**then retreated to her room an hour ago. I think she's asleep again. She sleeps so much these days.**

I set my phone down for a minute while I pulled my shirt off and changed into a pair of basketball shorts. It was too hot to stay in the jeans and T-shirt I wore to meet the girls.

I picked it up and typed out a response quicker than I could think about it.

**Me: What are you doing now?**

**Calli: Laying on my bed, texting you.**

Thoughts of Calli spread out on my bed as I devoured her pussy rushed through my mind and sent an electrical jolt straight to my dick.

**Me: You can't tell me you're laying on a bed…**

**Calli: Why not?**

**Me: Because I think naughty thoughts about it.**

**Calli: Like what?**

I took a deep breath, hoping it would force some oxygen into my brain.

**Me: I would spread your legs and eat your pussy.**

**Calli: Shit, I wish you were here.**

I laid down on my bed, adjusting myself and the rock-hard erection that desperately wanted her touch.

**Me: Me too, baby.**

**Calli: What else would you do if you were here?**

**Me: I would do whatever you wanted me to.**

**Calli: But what do YOU want to do? I want to hear what**

**turns you on.**

**Me: You turn me on, Calli. Everything about you is an instant boner-maker.**

**Me: If I were there, I would eat your pussy until you came on my tongue. Then I would get some ice and rub it across your nipples, loving how hard they get. I'd suck them and tease them until you come again.**

**Calli: I'm already getting wet just reading this.**

**Me: I'm hard as a fucking rock.**

**Calli: I would ride that for you and help you out if I could.**

I lowered my hand into my shorts and started stroking as I read her words. There was no way I was getting out of this conversation with her without coming.

**Me: Touch yourself, baby.**

**Calli: Okay.**

**Me: Think about my cock sliding deep inside of you, baby. Almost as deep as you took it down your throat. You're so good at taking my cock, aren't you, baby?**

**Calli: So good. You fit so well.**

**Me: Tell me how wet you are.**

**Calli: Really wet.**

I paused for a moment, not trusting that she was really touching herself. I knew that she had an iPhone like me, so without any hesitation, I opened the call window and pressed the button beside her name to FaceTime her.

It rang a few times, and I knew she was probably freaking out about me FaceTiming her.

"Hey," she finally answered, the phone pointed to the corner of the bedroom instead of at her. "I thought we were going to keep that going in the text message."

She laughed, but it was nervous laughter.

"We were, but I had a feeling that you were lying about touching yourself, and we can't have that. I know that I'm wound tighter than a fucking top right now, so if you're as sexually frustrated as me, then we're going to work this out between us. Which means I want to see you when you come so I know that you're not faking it. If I can't be there to take care of you, the least I can do is make sure you're taken care of over the phone."

"Oh, I'm fine. Really," she whispered as I heard her move around on the bed. Finally, a few seconds later, she turned the camera to face her.

"So, all that talk between us in those text messages didn't get you all hot and bothered?"

"It was hot…"

"But?"

"Nothing," she lied. She shook her head and looked away.

"Tell me how wet you are, Calli. Or better yet, show me."

"No!" she whisper-shrieked. "I can't do that!"

"Why not? You already told me in a text message that you were touching yourself. You weren't lying, were you?"

She squirmed as she looked everywhere but at me.

"There's nothing to be embarrassed about, baby. I wish I were there to watch you in person. I think it's fucking sexy that you play with yourself."

She chewed her lower lip and barely made eye contact with me.

"Do you want to see what you do to me?" I asked, hoping

this would make her more comfortable showing herself to me. I reached into my shorts again and pulled my cock out, stroking it as I lowered the phone to show her.

I watched as her eyes widened, but she refused to look away from the screen. She licked her lips and stared as I pumped it for her.

"You make me so fucking hard, baby."

She let out a small gasp as I spat into my hand and used it to wipe away the drop of pre-cum glistening on the tip. I stroked harder and faster, lowering the phone so he was the star of the show. I could still see her on the small screen as she watched with fascination as I jerked off for her.

"I want to fuck you so bad, Calli," I gritted. "I wish this was your pussy instead of my hand. You remember how tight she clenches around him, don't you, baby? The way she grips him and milks him for everything he has."

"Yes," she whispered, chewing on her lower lip again.

I wanted to be there so I could free it before claiming her mouth with mine.

"Do you want me to come for you, Calli?"

I gripped the base of my cock and stilled my hand, waiting for her to answer.

"Yes. Come, Dylan."

That was all it took. Those words on her lips.

I held the phone as steady as I could as I jerked mercilessly, picturing Calli's tits on the receiving end as I shot ropes of cum up my stomach.

"Fuckkkk," I groaned, letting my head fall back onto the pillow as I closed my eyes and tried to catch my breath.

"That was nothing compared to coming inside of you, but it

will have to do."

"That was hot…"

I opened my eyes and lifted the phone back to my face.

"Now it's your turn."

Her eyes widened as she started to look away.

"You don't have to if you don't want to, Calli. I would never ask you to do anything that you were uncomfortable with. I just want you to know that you can trust me. I wouldn't ever tell anyone that we did this, I just want you to feel good, too."

Her shoulders lifted with the deep breath she took.

"I trust you," she said softly.

I smiled, relieved when she returned it.

She shifted on the bed, and I could see her hand dip below the waistband of her shorts. I could hear the blood rushing past my ears as excitement to watch her washed over me.

She closed her eyes and lowered the camera but then stopped. I couldn't see what was happening because the camera was now aimed at the wall.

"Everything okay?" I asked.

She brought the phone back up to her face, which now had a scowl on it.

"My mom is up." She sighed heavily. "Sorry, I need to go check on her."

"Don't be sorry."

"I'll talk to you later?"

"Of course. Call me whenever you're free."

"Goodnight, Dylan."

"Goodnight, Calli."

She ended the call and I hated the nagging feeling that said she wasn't going to call me back tonight.

# Twenty-Six

## Calli

"Son of a bitch!" I turned away from the stove and grabbed a rag to wipe off the bacon grease that had splattered onto my arm.

"Are you alright?" Lucas asked, stepping closer to look at the burn.

"I'm fine," I sighed heavily. "Can you please take over the bacon? We're never going to get these dishes out if I don't stop burning it."

"I'm on it." He smiled and then yelled throughout the kitchen, passing out new assignments as he took over the lunch rush.

Today's popular menu item was macaroni and cheese with maple bacon crumbles. Everyone else was doing their part to get the food prepared, but no matter how hard I tried, I couldn't stop burning everything I touched.

I had tried working up front, but my focus wasn't there, leading to me messing up orders and causing more chaos in the kitchen. Deciding that I was useless to everyone today, I went to my office and closed the door.

Mom hadn't come with me today, but instead of having Paisley stay with her at home, one of her neighbors had asked her to come over and play cards for a while. She promised to call me if there were any problems but assured me that she and my mother used to spend hours drinking sweet tea and playing cards. Her doctor had assured me again that I didn't need to hover around her and that it was good for both of us if she went about doing things she used to do.

 I sat behind my desk, frowning when I went through my emails. There was nothing that had come through worth frowning about, other than a handful of spam ones, but my mood was sour, and no matter how hard I tried, I couldn't shake this mood.

"Hey, Lucas said you needed a break. Is everything okay?" Paisley asked, standing in the doorway. She was running the frontline and helping train a few new employees, so she hadn't been in the kitchen when I burned myself.

"Yeah, just having one of those days."

I didn't bother looking up at her because I didn't want my mood to rub off on her. I was better if I just stayed in my office and had as little interaction with people as possible.

"I'm sorry. Anything I can do to make it better?" she offered.

"No, but thank you. Just leave me to my misery."

"What about me? Is there anything I can do?"

My head whipped up as I spotted Dylan's head pop up beside Paisley's.

"I'll let you two talk," she said, ushering him inside my office before pulling the door closed behind her.

"Hey, what are you doing here?" I asked, standing up and coming around the desk to hug him.

He wrapped me in his arms and pulled me tight against his chest.

"I was waiting on the guys to get back with more supplies and thought I'd come down for lunch. I think they're so used to seeing me here all the time that they automatically just sent me back with Paisley."

I laughed but it felt hard and constricted.

"So, what's going on?"

"Nothing." I shook my head but refused to lift it from his chest. For once, I felt calm. "It's just been one of those days where everything that can go wrong does."

"I'm sorry. I hate those days."

"Me too."

I finally pulled away, brushing my arm where I burned myself against his side. I winced and hissed out a breath but didn't want to draw attention to it.

Dylan's eyes narrowed as he gently grabbed my wrist and turned my arm so he could see it.

"What happened?"

"I burned myself cooking bacon earlier. It's fine, just a little burn."

"It looks like it hurts. Did you put anything on it?"

I shook my head again. I'd had plenty of grease burns in my life to know that there wasn't much you could do for them other than wait it out and let them heal.

"You really should put something on it, Calli. Do you have any Vaseline?"

"Not with me. I already took some Tylenol. It'll be fine. Thank you, though."

"Do you have a first aid kit?" he asked.

"Yeah, it's in the kitchen."

He opened the door and walked out there like he owned the place.

"Hi, can someone point me to where the first aid kit is?"

I heard a few of the guys talking, and then a few minutes later, Dylan returned with the box of supplies and closed my office door again.

He opened it up, looked around, and smiled when he spotted what he was looking for.

"Aha! Bingo."

He pointed for me to sit and then pulled up a chair, resting my arm on the edge of my desk.

Without saying anything, he tore open the small packet of Vaseline and squirted some directly onto my burn without touching it. Then he grabbed another package and pulled out a thin piece of gauze that he set on top of it. A few minutes later, and some medical tape to hold it in place, and I was taken care of.

Or at least *my burn* was taken care of. The rest of me was aching for him to touch me more as his body brushed against mine. The way his leg was situated between mine so he could get closer made me want to reach across and trail my fingers over his body, sending goosebumps across his skin the way I did when I spent the night at his house.

That night was the best night of my life, and I hadn't forgotten a single detail about it. Not the way he looked when he came or the satisfied expression that lingered on his face after making me climax repeatedly.

My cheeks burned hot as the heat spread throughout me at the reminders of the things we did that night. My breathing had grown more rapid as well, my nipples hardening against the thin fabric of my bra while my panties got wetter by the second.

"Are you okay?" he asked lightly, a knowing smile on his face.

My eyes snapped back to his as I tried to regain my composure. I looked down to find that I had scooted as far off my chair as possible to get my crotch lined up with his knee, desperate for some friction where I needed it the most.

"Yeah. Of course," I said with a ragged breath. "Why wouldn't I be?"

"Oh, I don't know," he teased as he closed the first aid kit and looked at me. "Maybe because you were just about to hump my knee."

I gasped, my cheeks flaming with embarrassment again.

"I was not!"

He leaned back in his chair, his leg still painfully close to my throbbing pussy. Would it be such a terrible thing if I did hump his knee? Lord knew I had enough pent-up sexual frustration to make even the sanest person go crazy.

"I can help you with that before I go," he offered, subtly licking his lips.

"With what? I'm good. Totally good. Cool as a cucumber."

I fidgeted with the bottom of my tank top, hoping his eyes were focused on the delicate lace trim on the neckline and not my nipples that continued to give me away.

"Why do you push me away so much lately?" he asked, leaning close as he rested his elbows on his knees and lifted my chin with his finger. "You know that I can make you come, Calli. So why are you fighting it?"

My insides quivered as I thought about it.

"I don't know."

There—an honest answer.

"I don't want to push you into doing something you don't want to do, but I also don't mind having my lunch in here if you're okay with it."

There was a twinkle in his eye that I should have picked up on but didn't.

"Oh. Okay. Yeah. Sure. Do you know what you want? I can ask one of the guys to bring a plate back for you."

He pulled his lower lip between his teeth before letting his eyes roam down my body, fixating on the juncture between my thighs.

"There's no need for that," he said. "My food is already here."

"You can't be serious," I whispered, looking around the office even though there wasn't anyone else there but him and me.

"I sure am."

"But what if someone walks in?"

"Does your door lock?"

I nodded.

He winked and then got up and locked it.

"Problem solved."

"But what if they hear us?"

"Then I guess you'll have to be a good girl and stay quiet. Now get up on your desk so I can sit down and enjoy my lunch."

A chill spread through me as I saw the hungry look in his eyes. I took the hand he extended to me and stood up. I felt nervous about doing something like this when there were people on the other side who could hear us or, better yet— just know what we were doing behind closed doors.

But then Dylan pulled me against his body and wrapped his arms around my waist as his mouth lowered against mine. The kiss was soft and sweet, his way of reminding me that I knew him and trusted him. As he deepened the kiss, I started to feel the stress melt away, my arousal becoming more prominent.

He broke the kiss and nudged my head to the side with his before kissing along the side of my neck and nibbling my ear. Then I felt his hands slip down my waist and move to the front to work the button on my jean shorts. Within seconds, they were falling to the floor along with my panties.

He guided me to where he wanted me to sit on the desk and then spread my legs as he sat down and leaned forward.

"I could eat this pussy all day, every day."

Then he lowered his mouth to my lips and began his delicious torture.

I tried to stay quiet and found myself gripping his head as he used two fingers to fuck me while sucking my clit. I wanted to scream his name and make sure everyone knew that he was responsible for the orgasm that was pouring out of me.

My thighs trembled against his head as I felt the last spasm ripple through me.

He pulled away slowly, wiping his mouth with the back of his hand while looking up at me.

"You're too good at that," I joked, realizing that he had me coming in under five minutes.

"I know your body and what it likes."

"Well, it also likes your dick," I muttered, taking his hand as he helped me down. He was still sitting in my chair, a cocky grin spreading over his face.

"Is that so?"

"Very much so."

"We still have time." He wiggled his eyebrows.

I stood in front of him, wearing nothing but my tank top and bra, his hands leisurely roaming over my thighs.

This time, instead of being timid and afraid, I decided to go for what I wanted. I stepped closer and nodded to his crotch, where I could see the outline of his erection.

"Take him out."

His eyes stayed locked on mine while doing what I asked.

Once his cock sprung free, I found myself climbing on top of him in record time.

"Shit," he muttered, tipping his head back. "I don't have a condom."

I frowned, not wanting to stop.

"I'm clean and on the pill," I offered, chewing my nail nervously.

"I'm clean and not on any pills. Other than Ibuprofen," he joked.

I shook my head and lowered myself onto his lap, going slowly as he lined himself up at my entrance. I slid down, closing my eyes as I felt him going deeper inside me.

"Fuck," he breathed, pinching his eyes closed.

"What's wrong?"

"Nothing." He shook his head. "This feels so fucking good that I'm trying not to blow my load right away."

I giggled and began riding him slowly until I knew he was okay.

He tugged my shirt down enough to expose one breast and then the other. My bra was a thin black see-through material that seemed to drive him wild as he licked at it before attempting to suck a nipple into his mouth.

Finally, I reached up and pulled the cups down, freeing my breasts which were immediately cradled in his hands. He sucked hard, taking his time going back and forth between nipples.

I arched my back and ground my hips harder, building the friction we both needed.

"You feel so fucking good," he breathed, releasing my nipple for a split second.

"You too. I feel like I'm going to come again already."

"Touch yourself, Calli. Rub your clit while you come on my cock."

I nodded, this time not too shy to do what he asked. Maybe it was different because we weren't on the phone, and his dick was literally inside me. But I did as he asked and rubbed my clit the way I needed it, feeling the tingle creep up my spine.

"I'm going to come," I warned, panting as my breaths grew heavier.

I rode him harder, thrusting my hips forward while pushing myself over the edge.

My body trembled at the same time his fingers dug into my ass, and he clenched beneath me, shooting his load inside me.

Once we were done, we sat there resting our foreheads on each other's as we tried to catch our breath.

"I love you," he whispered.

My body froze, and I knew he could feel it because he started to pull away. He didn't look at me or question why I didn't say it back.

I knew Paisley would be coming back to check on us soon, so I got up and got dressed, Dylan following suit behind me. I felt like an ass for not talking about what just happened, but I also knew that I wasn't going to be able to say the words I knew he was hoping I would say.

I made sure we both looked decent and that all of our clothes were put on the right way before opening the door and finding Paisley heading our way.

"Thank you for lunch," Dylan said, giving me a quick peck

on the cheek before making his way through the kitchen and out the door. He was rushing to get out of there, and I couldn't blame him.

"What did he eat?" Colby asked another kid with a confused look on his face. "I didn't see him take any food back there."

"Get back to work," Lucas scolded, not daring to look me in the eye.

Paisley shook her head as her grin spread wider across her face.

"Oh, he ate alright."

"Shut up," I hissed, heading back to my office and closing the door. Thankfully she didn't follow me in because there was no way I could deny what had just happened in there.

# Twenty-Seven

## Dylan

"I didn't think you were going to be able to do it," Curtis said, shaking his head as he looked around at the work we had done. "And a few weeks early at that."

"I told you." I winked when he rolled his eyes at me.

"And it's not bad either," he added, walking around as he inspected the last roof.

"Of course it's not. I was in charge, and I only deliver the best."

"Except for in the bedroom, then that's where I reign supreme," Maverick said as he joined us. His team was getting ready to start the HVAC work now that we were done. All of the vent pipes had already been installed in the roof, so he was up there to ensure their work was done properly before giving them the green light to proceed with the rest.

"You wish," I muttered, my shoulders tightening when I thought about what he said. Calli seemed more than satisfied with me, but that still didn't stop the intrusive thoughts that were forcing their way in, wondering if Maverick would be the better lover if given a chance.

It wasn't that I doubted my abilities as a man to please a woman in the bedroom, but Maverick had far more experience with it than me. Hell, he could probably make someone come just from looking at her the right way. He didn't boast about his sexual abilities, other than when taking jabs at someone, but we all knew that he was never lacking when it came to sex.

Maverick wasn't a *settle-down* kind of guy. Everyone in town—and the neighboring towns—knew that. He built his reputation on being a handyman, and when they said *handy,* they meant it. He had broken more hearts than anyone could count, but the one thing that was consistent with him was that he never led anyone on to think there could be more. He was clear with his intentions, which set him apart from everyone else.

Curtis went on about the next project we would be starting next week, but my mind was scattered, unable to focus.

"She's gotten that far under your skin, hasn't she?" Maverick asked, nudging me with his elbow as we walked behind Curtis.

"Who?" I asked dumbly, thankful we were heading into cooler temperatures and that it wasn't blistering hot up on the roof. We were still having a hotter September than usual, but I was hopeful that it would change soon.

"You know who."

I shrugged, not wanting to admit anything.

"You don't have to say anything, but it's written on your face."

"What about you?" I asked, deferring the conversation to him. "Have you talked to Paisley lately?"

He shrugged and looked around, making a note in his phone before putting it back into his pocket.

"We've talked a few times when I've gone in for lunch."

"Are you going to ask her out?"

"I don't know," he sighed. "Probably not."

I frowned and stopped walking. While Maverick wasn't the settle-down, relationship type of guy, he wasn't usually an asshole to women, either.

"Why not?"

He looked at me and then looked away.

"Because," he said slowly. "I kind of like her. She's different than the other girls I talk to."

I tipped my head back and laughed.

"And that's a problem why?"

"I don't know. It just is." His brown eyes pinned me with a look that said he didn't want to get into it. "I don't do the whole relationship thing."

"Has she said that's what she wants?"

"No. But have you ever met a woman who *doesn't* want that?"

"No," I agreed. "But I've also never met anyone like Paisley. She knows what she wants and isn't afraid to go after it. If she hasn't hinted at wanting a relationship, then maybe don't assume she's looking to trap you."

"You make it sound so easy," he laughed.

"It is. You talk to people, figure out what everyone wants, and then you work together to make it happen. Easy peasy."

"And that's what's happening between you and Calli? You're *both* opening up and telling the other what you want so you can *both* make it happen?"

My jaw tightened as I kept my head looking forward. I knew that if I looked at Maverick, I would see the same truth in his eyes that I heard in his words. I hadn't told anyone about how I had told Calli I loved her, only to have her not respond. I was too embarrassed by it but even worse, I didn't want to think about what it meant for us and our relationship—if we even had one at this point.

"Shut up," I said, elbowing him in the side like he did to me earlier. "Our situation is different."

"Why's that?"

I could hear the change in his tone and knew that he was asking with sincerity, not to mock me.

"I have no fucking clue," I muttered, picking up the pace to keep up with Curtis before I completely missed everything he said.

# Twenty- Eight

## Calli

"Why don't you ask Dylan out tonight?" Paisley asked, sitting on the island as I worked on basting the short ribs before taking them out to the smoker.

"Because I need to be here with Mom." I looked into the living room to find her sitting in the recliner that Dad used to love, wrapped with a blanket even though it was hot today. I was used to the constant heat in Florida, but the locals were constantly griping about how we were having a hotter than usual September and how they couldn't wait for it to cool off. Thankfully it was already cooler than the past few months, so I wasn't going to complain.

"I can stay with her. It's not like I have any plans." Paisley pouted, swinging her legs in front of her.

"Call Maverick, ask him out."

"Nope. Can't do that."

"Why not?"

"Because I'm waiting for him to ask *me* out."

"It's not the 1920s, Pais. You can ask a guy out. It's the cool new thing to do, and spoiler alert—they love it." I brushed the ribs with another coating of the sweet chili glaze and then pulled the foil up around them.

"I know that I *can*. I just don't want to. *If* Maverick wants to ask me out, then he can do so. It doesn't matter any to me."

"Is that why you're sitting there pouting? Because it doesn't matter?"

"I'm not pouting," she said with a sigh. "I'm just saying it would be great *if* I had plans, but I'm quickly learning that there's not much to do in a small town on the weekend."

I pulled my lips together into a line and tried to fight back the tears. This week had been more challenging than usual for me, and I found myself regretting so much about my past. Now hearing that Paisley wasn't happy here was the last straw.

I took a slow, steadying deep breath, grabbed the tray, and headed outside to the smoker. She hopped off the counter and followed me, quietly closing the door behind her.

"What's going on?" she asked, staying out of the way as I set the foil packets inside.

"Nothing," I lied, closing the lid and wishing I had something else to keep me busy and distracted.

"You're such a terrible liar." She folded her arms over her chest and stared at me.

"I don't know what I'm doing!" I flung my arms at my side helplessly. "I'm screwing everything up, and now you hate it here."

"I don't hate it here," she assured me, her eyes softening. "And you're not screwing anything up."

"Yes I am." I sniffed, trying to will my tears not to come down my face.

"Oh yeah? Like what?"

"Everything, Pais. Things with my mother aren't going how I thought they would. The restaurant is busier than I can handle, but I don't have time to focus on that because I'm worried about my mom. Things with Dylan—it's just all too much."

I let my head fall back as I closed my eyes so I didn't have to see the pity in her eyes as she looked at me.

"Hey," she said, shaking my arm to get me to look at her.

"You're not screwing things up. Your mom is fine. This is all normal and what the doctor said to expect. You're doing your best, and no one thinks otherwise. The restaurant is doing well, and the newbies should be trained soon. You're doing great with running your own business, Calli. Be proud of that."

I let out a shaky breath and opened my eyes, now filled with tears.

"This is all so much harder than I thought it would be," I sniffled.

"I know it is. But you have me here to help you. It's going to be okay." She squeezed my hands gently. "Now, what's going on with Dylan?"

"Nothing, but I'm sure that will change soon when he realizes that he fell for a girl who can't love him how he deserves to be loved."

"Why not?"

"Because it's too much, Paisley."

"Loving him is too much?" She furrowed her brow. "How so?"

"Because he deserves so much more than I can give him." I threw my hands up in the air. "I can't even find the time to go on a date with him because I need to be here for Mom. He's been patient with me so far, but you and I both know that will only last for a little while. Then he'll decide that he's had enough and leave."

She shook her head sympathetically. This was exactly what I *didn't* want to see from her.

"You're wrong," she said softly.

"No, I'm not. There's not enough of me to go around for everyone, Paisley. If I let myself fall for Dylan, I'm going to fall hard because I think I might already be in love with him. Never mind the fact that he already said it to me, and I couldn't bring myself to say it back. But that's neither here nor there, and it doesn't matter because I can't be in love right now. Being in love means spending all your time with that person and building a life together, but my life is my mom right now. I came here to help take care of her and be there for her. It's the least I can do after moving to Florida and not getting to see my dad before he passed. I don't want to lose my mom and regret not being there for her too." My voice cut out as the raw emotion consumed me, my body shaking as I cried.

Paisley wrapped her arms around me and hugged me as I fell apart.

# Twenty-Nine

## Dylan

After not seeing Calli in over two weeks, I started to worry that she had ghosted me. Since I was done working at the new strip mall and had been moved to a new job on the other side of town, I couldn't sneak in and see her on my lunch like I used to. We texted here and there, but the messages were short and seemed to lack effort on her end. It was almost like she was trying to give the bare minimum so I would walk away and leave her alone.

It was after ten on a Friday night, and I was throwing back tequila like it was water and I was stranded in the desert. Not a wise idea, but I'd done worse. I had my phone out, scrolling through social media, when I came across a blog post from Spill The Beans, Maggie's romance advice column. She'd recently branched out and decided to have a presence online, which was bad news for me tonight.

Before I could talk myself out of it, I clicked the link to the blog page and started a new message.

*Dear Ask Mags,*

*Hi. It's me again. The one man who can't seem to stop falling in love with women who don't want to love him back. Don't worry, this time I'm not coming to you because I'm in love with my best friend again. This time it's worse than that.*

*I found a woman who stole my breath—not in a literal way. It's not like she was a terrible kisser and I couldn't breathe while we made out. She's a fantastic kisser, by the way. Really knows what she's doing and even has this little trick that she does that drives me crazy.*

*Not crazy in a bad way—though I think I'm heading there too. But crazy in a good way. In such an amazing way that I fell in love with her without even trying. She's the sun to my moon or to my stars or maybe to a planet? I don't really know. But I think I want to orbit around her and save her from any sort of meteor attacks.*

*I mean, I know that's hard because you can't stop a meteor, but I would die trying for her. Not that I'm coming to you with a death wish or anything—it's not like that. I'm just saying I would do whatever I could for her. Does that make sense? Probably not.*

*Where was I?*

*Oh yeah. I love her, but she doesn't love me back. She's ghosting me, and I don't know why. Am I so unlovable that no one wants to be with me? I mean, LL Cool J wasn't lying when he said he needed love, and guess what? So do I.*

*But why can't I find it? And more importantly—why are pizzas round, but the box they come in is square? I know that's not related to what we're talking about, but it's been weighing on my mind for a while now, and I'd really like the answer.*

*If you know, please reply back and tell me. Why doesn't she love me, and why is the pizza not the same shape as the box?*

*Sincerely,*

*Unlovable Pizza Lover*

I tossed my phone onto the couch and let myself sink lower, thankful I didn't press send.

*************************************

I had no clue what time it was, but the light burned my eyes as I looked around to find my phone as it rang from somewhere close by.

My head throbbed as I tried to wake up, surprised to find myself still on the couch and not in bed. The ringing finally stopped, and I was going to give up locating my phone until it started again.

I tried really hard to focus on where it was coming from as I slid my hand across the couch cushions. Finally, I found it in between the cushions and retrieved it. The call ended by the time I got it out, but the caller ID showed the missed calls were from Maggie, which meant she would be calling again in a matter of seconds. *Just great.*

"Ugh," I grunted as I answered it and held the phone to my ear.

"You sound like you're feeling mighty fine this morning," she teased, though I had no idea how she knew I would be this hungover.

"It was a long night," I muttered, forcing myself to sit up right.

"I can imagine."

"Why do you say that?"

"Oh, no reason, *unlovable pizza lover.*"

I frowned as fuzzy memories tried to shove their way back into my head. I shook it, trying to clear the fog, when I remembered going to her blog page last night.

"Fuck. Please tell me I didn't send that to you."

"You sure did. And I believe the saying you were looking for is that she's your sun, your moon, and all of your stars. However, given the turn the email took, it could also be taken as a medieval political theory in which she is the only source of her own light, and you're the moon which merely reflects lights and has no value without the sun. Either way, there seems to be astrological love involved."

"I don't think so. The only love out there is my one-sided love for her," I muttered, shifting as I pulled a remote control out from under my ass.

"Oh, Dylan, what happened?"

"I don't know. I fell in love and thought she felt the same way, but I've hardly talked to her in two weeks. Pretty much ever since I told her that I loved her," I lowered my voice as the embarrassment crept over me.

I could hear sniffling on the other end of the line and pressed the phone closer to my ear.

"Are you crying?" I asked, knowing that Maggie had the biggest heart of anyone I'd ever met and she was "love's" biggest fan.

"No," she lied, blowing her nose.

"You're as bad of a liar as Calli."

"It's not fair," she said angrily into the phone.

"That I called you a liar?"

"No, that you love her, and she won't say it back, you big ol' dummy. Why didn't you tell us about this sooner? Two weeks is a long time to keep something like this from your best friends, you jerk."

"Wow. You really know how to cheer people up, Mags. You should start an inspirational and uplifting blog where you help people with your kind words of encouragement," I teased, happy to deflect.

"Shut up," she laughed. "You know that I love you."

"At least someone does."

"Oh, stop it. I know it sucks right now, but you cannot tell me that you honestly believe you're unlovable."

"Aren't I though? I mean, tell me I'm wrong, but I seem to fall for the ones who can't love me back. First, there was Ramona. Now Calli. What's next? Is the universe going to tempt me into falling for you, another best friend who's already taken?"

"Ramona doesn't count, and neither do I. We love you the same way you love us, and that will never change. The love you have for Calli is different. It's something I've never seen with you before, Dylan. So, stop disregarding it as if it isn't there."

"Why not? It would be so much easier to pretend that I didn't love her when she doesn't love me back."

"Because love is full of challenges! If it were easy, it wouldn't be worth it."

I chewed the inside of my cheek for a moment while I thought about that.

"But should it really be this hard?" I asked.

"That all depends on you."

"What does that mean?"

"It means that it's up to you and how much work you're willing to put into making this work. Are you going to sit on your couch and drink tequila until you pass out and send hilarious messages to my blog, or are you going to man up and go get the girl you love? You're the only one who can decide this, Dylan. One way or another, you're the only one responsible for your future and whether Calli is in it."

"I think you're giving me too much credit if you think that I'm going to be able to make Calli fall in love with me. If I haven't already, then there's really no hope for the future."

"Do you really think she doesn't love you?" Maggie questioned.

"She didn't say it back when I said it, and then she ghosted me shortly after."

"And you think that means she doesn't love you?"

"What else could it mean?"

"Gah, boys are so stupid sometimes," she muttered in frustration.

"Really, Mags, you need to get that inspirational site up and running ASAP. I can't be the only one who benefits from these uplifting messages."

"Oh, stop it. I mean you're being stupid because you're so stuck in your head right now that you're fixating on the fact that she didn't say she loves you back when you should be considering that she *does* love you and that it scares her to admit it."

*Fuck.*

I laid my head back against the couch cushion and rubbed at my temple with my free hand. Why hadn't I considered that?

"You don't have to say it," she replied cheerfully. "I know that I'm right."

"And a huge pain in my ass," I muttered sarcastically.

"The best pain in your ass you could ever ask for. Now pull yourself together and figure out a way to get your girl. If you need some help, I can whip up some banana nut—"

"No," I interrupted. "I don't need help with my stamina, Maggie. Trust me; we're fine in that department."

"Well, if you change your mind, you know where to find me."

"Thanks."

"Anytime. Keep me posted on what happens?"

"Will do. Thanks for calling, and sorry for sending that to your blog last night. Please delete it, and let's never speak of it again."

"Nope, no can do. I'm printing it as we speak. I'm taking it to our next weekly dinner so I can show Ramona."

"You're so mean," I grumbled, knowing how much Ramona

would enjoy reading it.

"Yeah, but you love me. Talk to you later."

I hung up the phone and allowed myself a few minutes to rest before getting up to wash last night's tequila off of me.

# Thirty

## Calli

I woke up sore from sleeping in the hospital chair beside my mom's bed last night. She had fallen while I was out running errands this morning and Paisley called to let me know they were taking her by ambulance.

The doctors wanted to watch her overnight to make sure she was okay before releasing her. I had sat on pins and needles while waiting for the results of her tests to come back, praying that there were no serious injuries. Paisley stayed with me until around eleven, when I was finally able to send her home. She'd asked if I wanted her to call Dylan for me, but I declined.

It wasn't that I *didn't* want to talk to Dylan; it was that it was too hard. Things were too complicated in my life to allow myself to fall even harder for him. There was no way I could run a restaurant, care for my mom, and make a relationship work. He deserved better than that, even if it hurt to admit.

"How's she doing?" the doctor asked quietly as he stood at the end of her bed.

"She seems good. Sleeping a lot."

He nodded and gave her a sympathetic smile.

"Well, the good news is that her tests returned normal, so we don't need to keep her for additional monitoring. She's a bit dehydrated, which might be why she fell. Her urine sample confirmed that when she was first brought in, but having her on an IV has helped."

I bent forward and pressed my face into my hands.

"I'm sorry. I make sure that she has water and try to confirm that she's drinking it throughout the day, but it's hard to tell whether it's the same bottle I've given her from the start or if she's refilled it."

"You have nothing to be sorry for."

He grabbed the chair from the corner and pulled it close to where I was sitting.

"Calli, can I talk to you for a minute about your mom's condition?"

"Of course," I said, lifting my head and pulling my shoulders back. He was going to tell me just how much I was failing with taking care of her; I just knew it.

"I understand that you're her caretaker and you're doing a great job."

"But…" I sighed heavily, just waiting for it.

"But the level of care that your mother needs far exceeds what you're able to do while running your own business."

I lowered my head and nodded.

"I don't know what to do," I admitted, the overwhelming feeling of defeat washing over me.

"I'm not saying that you're not doing the best you can, Calli. I'm saying that her dementia is progressing quickly and that you need help. Both of you do."

"Okay," I pulled in a deep breath. I needed to keep myself together for Mom. "What do you propose we should do?"

"My recommendation would be either to bring in help through in-home care services or to transition her to a nursing home where they can provide care for her 24 hours a day.

There's one in Whiskey Mountain that I strongly recommend, as well as a new one that just opened in Fallen Oaks."

I looked at my mom and felt the burning sting of tears in my eyes.

"I can't move her out of her house. That's her home. That's where she and my dad spent their lives together until he passed. I can't ask her to walk away and leave all of that behind."

"I understand. It's hard to make these decisions, and I won't push you one way or another, but I do want to remind you that as this disease progresses, she may lose those memories that you hold dear. To you, that will always be the house that your parents shared special moments together in, but to her, it may become a house that she may not remember at all."

"So, you think it would be better to move her into a nursing home?" I asked, hating the way the words sounded coming out of my mouth. I promised my dad at his funeral that I would move here and take care of Mom, but was I really doing that if I was so quick to give up and put her in a nursing home?

"I think she needs a level of care that you can't provide without quitting your job and taking care of her 24/7."

I swallowed hard, the rising bile burning my throat.

I looked from him back to her and let the first tear fall without wiping it away.

"Give it some thought but don't feel like you have to rush to make a decision," he said as he stood up. "We're here to support you and your mom, so please let us know how we can help."

"Thank you."

I tried smiling, but it fell flat, so I gave up and returned my focus to my mom as the doctor walked out and closed the door behind him.

I lowered my head to her side of the bed and cried into the blanket. This was harder than I could have ever imagined, and I was stuck having to make a decision I didn't want to make. The emotions rolled over me in waves, and no matter how hard I tried, I couldn't force them to go away.

The door opened again, and I quickly wiped my face with the palms of my hand, desperate to get rid of the proof of my undoing. I turned my head, assuming the doctor had returned or a nurse was coming in to collect Mom's vitals. But standing there instead was Dylan.

"What are you doing here?" I asked, noticing the concern on his face as he approached me holding a to-go bag from Spill The Beans along with a tray filled with drinks.

"Paisley called me."

"Of course she did," I sighed with a laugh.

"Is it okay that I'm here?"

He seemed so timid and afraid, making me deeply regret how I'd been keeping him at a distance lately.

I nodded, too overwhelmed with emotion again to speak. I lowered my head, feeling the tears slide down my face.

He set the items on the table beside me, and then I felt his hand on my elbow, lifting me up. I couldn't bring myself to look at him, to know he was seeing me at my absolute worst.

But Dylan didn't seem to care. He just wrapped his arms around me and provided the comfort and safe place I needed to fall apart against his chest. I gripped his shirt tightly as everything I had been holding in for weeks finally came spilling out.

"Shhh, it's okay," he whispered, rubbing his hands up and down my back.

A few minutes later, I was a snotty mess and accepted the tissues he handed me so I could clean my face before looking at him. I was surprised that my mom had slept through all of this, but her soft snores were comforting, knowing she wasn't witnessing me falling apart.

"I'm sorry," I apologized, grabbing a few more tissues to wipe his shirt.

He lifted my chin with his finger, forcing me to look at him.

"You don't get to apologize to me, Calli."

"I feel like it's necessary," I laughed. "I made a mess out of your shirt."

"I don't care about the shirt. All that I care about is you."

My heart swelled at his words as the words I needed to say tickled my lips.

"I love you, Dylan."

He looked shocked by it for half a second before his grin spread across his face.

"I should have told you a while ago when you first said it to me, and I'm sorry for that. I just couldn't bring myself to say it because I thought you deserved better than me, and hell, you probably still do. I'm a hot mess, and I don't know how to do the whole dating thing while caring for my mom and trying to run a business. So yeah, maybe you deserve someone who can make the time for you, but she won't love you like I do becau—"

"No more talking," he interrupted before closing his mouth over mine.

My body immediately betrayed me, and all of the fight I had left to prove that we shouldn't be together vanished.

"But," I objected, pulling away for a quick second before his hand rested against the back of my head and held me in place.

"No," he murmured against my lips.

I felt the giggles bubble up inside me as I kissed him back.

Finally confident that I wouldn't talk any more nonsense, he let go of my head and stepped back so we could both catch our breath.

"I brought you a honey lavender latte and an apple crumble muffin. Maggie said you've ordered those several times, so I figured it was a safe bet."

"You brought me coffee," I said dumbly, accepting the cup he offered.

"And breakfast," he added, nodding for me to sit down before he handed me the muffin.

"Are you eating too?"

"Yeah, Maggie packed a banana nut muffin for me. I grabbed a few extra in case your mom was up and wanted something besides hospital food."

"Thank you, Dylan. That was very sweet of you. All of this is just so…."

"Sweet?" he offered with a wink.

"Yes, very sweet. But I didn't do anything to deserve this. If anything, I wouldn't blame you for not speaking to me again after I practically ghosted you."

"I won't lie; that sucked. But a very wise person told me that if I love something, I need to fight for it. And Calli, you're very much worth it. I will fight for you for as long as I live if you just give me a chance to show you that I can be there for you. For both of you." He looked at my mom and smiled.

"I know you don't want me to apologize, but I still feel like I need to. I just got overwhelmed and couldn't figure out how to do all this. It felt like I was failing and I didn't want that for us. For you."

"I know. I get it, Calli. I can't imagine how much pressure has been on you to do everything, but I promise you that I'm here to help. Whatever you need, you just tell me."

I worried my lower lip between my teeth.

"The doctor thinks my mom needs more care than I can provide. He recommended either having someone come in for in-house health care or that I put her in a nursing home where she has access to care 24/7."

"How do you feel about that?" he asked gently.

"I feel like no matter what decision I make, I'm failing her." Another tear slid down my face.

"Well, let's just take it one day at a time. You don't have to make a decision right now. Let's focus on getting her home, then we can return to this conversation later."

I nodded, the tears burning the back of my throat too much to want to talk. We sat there quietly, eating our muffins and sipping our lattes.

"Did they say when she'll be discharged and able to go home?" he asked a few minutes later, breaking the silence as we finished our food.

"Her tests came back normal, so I'm guessing they'll be working on her discharge paperwork soon. He said there was no reason to keep her for monitoring."

"Okay, cool." He nodded, clearly thinking through something without saying what it was.

"You don't have to wait around here, though. You can go if you want to. I'll be fine getting her home."

He glanced at his watch and then back to me.

"I have a few errands that I need to run, but I'll call you in a little bit to check in. Is that okay?"

I nodded and smiled, finally not feeling the strain of faking it.

He pecked me on the lips and then headed out. I sat back in my chair, staring at my mom while praying that the right answer about what to do for her would come to me.

# Thirty-One

## Dylan

I stood in Calli's kitchen, nervous as hell as I worried that this was a terrible plan.

"It's fine. Stop worrying," Paisley scolded, leaning against the counter as she finished highlighting the calendar she was working on.

"What if she hates it?"

"She won't."

"But I didn't ask first."

"You led with your heart. That's all that matters," Maggie said as she walked in, carrying another armful of casserole dishes that she loaded into the freezer.

"Don't be so scared," Ramona teased, bumping her hip into mine before stocking the K-cups into the organizer we had bought. "Everything is going to be just fine."

I inhaled deeply and let it out slowly.

But then I heard keys in the front door and started to panic again.

"Stop it!" all three women scolded before Maggie opened the door.

Patti was the first to come in and looked as shocked as I imagined she would be when she saw the four of us in her kitchen.

"Oh my goodness," she said, holding her hand to her heart.

"You brought me daisies again!"

I grinned stupidly at the giant bouquet I'd assembled for her with Paisley's help.

"What's going o—" Calli said but stopped when she spotted us. "Oh, hi!" She waved nervously, looking around as she tried to figure out what was happening.

I grabbed the flowers from the island and took them to Patti, unsure if she remembered me. But the way she smiled before pulling me in for a hug was reassuring.

"Thank you for the beautiful flowers. What a treat to come home to."

"You're very welcome. I'm so happy you're feeling better."

Patti brushed her finger over my cheek before heading into the kitchen. She said hi to Paisley and then waited for her to introduce her to Maggie and Ramona.

"Hey, what's all this?" Calli asked softly as she stepped beside me and wrapped her arms around my waist. I cuddled her against me and loved the feeling of having her there.

"We all wanted to do something to help. I hope you don't mind, but I talked to Paisley and Maggie about what was happening, and things kinda just went from there."

Paisley gave me a wink before leading Patti to the back patio, where a few of her friends were waiting for her.

"Dylan asked for help with recipe ideas and then told me what was going on," Maggie explained. "I know you're not used to small-town life, but one thing about it is that we take care of each other. We're one giant family, so when we say you're not going through this alone, we mean it."

I kissed Calli's head when I noticed the tears in her eyes again.

"My friend's mom runs the town's food chain, meaning that when someone is in need, we rally together, and everyone prepares a dish. I spent the afternoon collecting them, and they're all packed up in your freezer with dates, heating instructions, and a little pick-me-up note from the person who made it. We didn't leave anything out for tonight since Dylan said he's got that covered."

Maggie winked at me, but I shook my head, not wanting to get into the debate again over whether I could grill for dinner tonight without burning the food. It had happened *one time.*

"I also baked some muffins and assorted breakfast breads, so you guys will have ready-to-eat options. I'll come by next week and bring some fresh goodies, but let me know if there's anything you want in particular. Since we're heading into fall, I'll be adding some pumpkin and apple items to the menu at Spill The Beans, but I'm happy to bring some here too."

"Thank you so much. That's too kind of you," Calli said, accepting the tissue Ramona handed her. "This is all too much!"

"It's not at all," Ramona said. "Now, I might not make delicious muffins, but I know good coffee, so I wanted to make sure you had some here too. Dylan told me your Keurig recently broke, so we all pitched in and got you the Keurig K-Café Single Serve Coffee, Latte & Cappuccino Maker. It may not make the over-the-top delicious drinks that Maggie makes, but it is definitely better than the crappy coffee Dylan makes at home."

"Hey now," I objected. "I'm a busy man; gotta have something quick and easy."

"Don't worry. I'll share some of my fancy coffee with you."

"We stocked you up on a variety of options," Ramona said, opening and closing the drawers of the organizer to show Calli the K-cups. "And we chose one that was safe for your mom, so you didn't have to worry about her burning herself on a hot pot of coffee."

"Thank you, I appreciate that."

Paisley came back inside, closing the patio door behind her.

"Where's Mom?" Calli asked, pulling away with a concerned look splashed across her face.

"She's outside with the girls." Paisley smiled, pulling Calli in for a hug.

"Girls? What girls?"

"Her friends," Paisley said softly. "Rita from across the street rallied the girls together. It turns out that they used to get together a few times a week to play cards, but it stopped shortly after your dad passed. When I told them what was happening, they all stepped in and wanted to help."

"Okay," Calli sighed, shaking her head. "What does that mean?"

Paisley grabbed Calli's hand and led her to the calendar on the fridge.

"It means that family takes care of each other, and we're all family, Calli. We know how important Cravings is to you, but we also know that your mom needs care 24/7 and that you can't do both."

"I know, bu—"

"BUT," Paisley interrupted. "You don't have to do all of this on your own, Calli. That's what we're saying. Everyone is rallying around you guys right now because we see that you need help, and that's nothing to be ashamed of. You're doing an amazing job with Mom, don't ever second guess yourself. But when you moved out here to take care of her, there was no way you knew what to expect. Neither of us did."

Calli covered her mouth as a sob escaped her throat.

"We've got this," Paisley assured her, squeezing an arm around her shoulders. "Aside from the meals that have been brought over, we also have a schedule going. I'll keep track of this and help you update it every month. But for now, we're all set. You'll see everyone's name on the right side, highlighted in their color. Then on the calendar, it shows who will be staying with Mom on those days. The ladies have taken the days during the week while you're at work and will take turns coming every day. You'll be home most evenings; however, you'll see the spots where I've added myself to stay the night."

I felt my stomach tighten as I worried about how Calli was going to handle all of these decisions being made for her.

"Why are you staying over those nights?" Calli asked quietly, her body stiffening.

"Because those are the nights you're going to take a break and stay with Dylan. I know you're afraid this can't work because it's all too much, but we've got this."

"And I'll be staying over here a few nights a week, too," I added, coming to stand on the other side of her. "I'm not coming to take advantage of being in your room. I'm coming so I can be on night duty those nights so you can get some sleep. I'll camp out on the couch, and you won't even notice I'm here."

Calli turned toward me, eyes filled with tears again.

"I can't believe you put all this together, Dylan."

"Are you mad?" I asked quietly, pulling my mouth to the side.

"No," she laughed, wrapping her arms behind my head.

"Not at all. The only thing I'm mad about is that it took me so long to tell you I love you."

"Well, there's no need to worry about the past, my love," I assured her, resting my forehead against hers. "We have the rest of our lives to make sure we tell each other how much we love them."

# Epilogue

## Calli

*Three Months Later*

"The snow is really coming down. You better go if you want to make it home before the roads freeze," I said, looking out the living room window.

My mom had already gone to bed after dinner, which had quickly become the new norm for her. Dylan spent most nights with us, except for the prescheduled ones where Paisley kicked me out of my own house once a week to give me a break.

I was pleasantly surprised by how well things were going and even more so with how much pressure had been lifted from my shoulders with everyone helping out. The ladies loved spending their time with Mom during the week, and instead of only one of them coming per day, all four of them would show up, and the Feisty Five, as I called them, would spend the day laughing and having fun.

Mom still had her ups and downs, but now that I had so much support, we were able to set up a routine that worked for everyone.

"I don't want to leave you and your mom by yourselves in the storm," Dylan said quietly, wrapping his arms around my waist and pressing his hands firmly against my stomach.

"We'll be fine. It's just snow."

Not that I had much experience with snow until now. Living in Florida was nice because we didn't get this bitter-cold weather, but I wasn't sure which I disliked more—having to worry about alligators sneaking up on me or shoveling snow and ice.

"You don't know how bad these storms can get. We might lose power." He leaned down and kissed behind my ear.

"I have candles," I giggled, leaning into his touch.

"Yeah, but what about food? How are you going to feed my little peanut? You know she gets hangry."

"We don't know that it's a girl," I laughed as he tickled my sides.

He moved around and kneeled in front of me, lifting the bottom of my hoodie before lowering the waistband of my sweats. He closed his eyes and kissed my stomach, already so in love with our baby.

"What if I'm not worried about the storm, and I don't doubt you can feed yourself if the power goes out," he said softly. "What if I just don't want to leave?"

"Then don't," I said a little too eagerly.

He stood up, lifted me to his hips, and grabbed my ass.

"Move in with us," I whispered in his ear.

It wasn't the first time I'd asked, but he wanted to take things slowly so we didn't disrupt the routine we had going for Mom.

"Do you think it's too soon for her?"

I shook my head and cupped his face in my hands.

"She's already used to having you here as it is. It wouldn't be that much different if you moved in."

"That means we can't sneak off to my house to have loud, crazy sex anymore," he whispered.

"True. But I've learned to be quiet… for the most part." I giggled when he nipped my ear.

"So, what do you say?" I pressed, sighing heavily as I waited for his answer. "Will you move in with us?"

He nodded and squeezed my ass harder before carrying me down the hallway to *our* bedroom.

**********

Ready to see what's happening with Paisley and Maverick? Be sure to grab their book here:

https://books2read.com/u/mllEOP

Looking for more small-town romance? Here are some books that you might enjoy!

Just One Time (Beaumont Creek Book 1)—A friends-to-lovers steamy romance!

https://books2read.com/u/3G52zK

'Til Death Do Us Part (Haven Brook Book 1)—A friends-to-lovers steamy romantic suspense!

https://books2read.com/u/m2RJNR

# Other Books By Samantha Baca

## **The Haven Brook Series (small-town romantic suspense):**

'Til Death Do Us Part (Haven Brook Book 1)

https://books2read.com/u/m2RJNR


The Cradle Will Fall (Haven Brook Book 2)

https://books2read.com/u/b6O0QE


The Ties That Bind (Haven Brook Book 3)

https://books2read.com/u/mqgoz8


A Very Haven Christmas (Haven Brook Book 4- Novella)

https://books2read.com/u/mvqGjj


Three Strikes, You're Gone (Haven Brook Book 5)

https://books2read.com/u/mvqL2z

## <u>The Dark Shadows Trilogy (romantic suspense)</u>

Five Steps Ahead (Dark Shadows Book 1)

https://books2read.com/u/38Q0gO

Ten Seconds Too Late (Dark Shadows Book 2)

https://books2read.com/u/3JRgVB

Against The Clock (Dark Shadows Book 3)

https://books2read.com/u/m2YwoR

## <u>The Stone Creek Series (small-town- novellas)</u>

Chocolate Covered Mistletoe (Stone Creek Book 1)

https://books2read.com/u/3LRk9N

Candy Coated Promises (Stone Creek Book 2)

https://books2read.com/u/mldP5Y

Pumpkin Spiced Possibilities (Stone Creek Book 3)

https://books2read.com/u/bojdwV

# **Beaumont Creek Series (small town)**

Just One Time (Beaumont Creek Book 1)

https://books2read.com/u/3G52zK


Second Chances (Beaumont Creek Book 2)

https://books2read.com/u/4Aj6Z0


Third Time's The Charm (Beaumont Creek Book 3)

https://books2read.com/u/b5lEyG


Four-ever Single (Beaumont Creek Book 4)

https://books2read.com/u/4j5jMX


Fifth Wheel (Beaumont Creek Book 5)

https://books2read.com/u/4XwKwa

# **Whiskey Mountain Series (small-town- novellas)**

Something To Talk About

https://books2read.com/u/4X62ag

Something To Think About

https://books2read.com/u/3GWAan

Something To Believe In

https://books2read.com/u/3yVzgB

Something To Live For

*Preorder link coming soon*

# **Sugarplum Falls Series (Holiday Novellas- can be read as standalone)**

Blame It On The Mistletoe

https://books2read.com/u/bw1rqe

Blame It On The Eggnog

https://books2read.com/u/38PPY6

Blame It On The Candy Canes (coming 11/3/23)

https://books2read.com/u/31DNo7

Blame It On The Blizzard (coming 11/17/23)

https://books2read.com/u/b6z6XE


## **Standalone Books**

One Last Wish

https://books2read.com/u/mqg7D9


Finding Love In Apartment 2C (novella)

https://books2read.com/u/bze9aZ

Cocky Counsel: A Hero Club Novel

https://books2read.com/u/31Kzkn


All Is Fair In Food And War (novella)

https://books2read.com/u/bp8qjX


## **Holiday Books (novellas)**

Snow Place To Go

https://books2read.com/u/4A560N

A Christmas Wish

https://books2read.com/u/4EKXpE

Holiday Hijinks

https://books2read.com/u/4DP6Ze

# Acknowledgments

Sometimes I stop and think about how lucky I am that I have the most incredible readers who love my books so much! Thank you for giving my book a chance. I know you have an abundance of options to choose from, and I'm honored that you picked mine. I hope you enjoyed it!

None of this would be possible without the help of my trusted alpha and beta readers. You ladies go above and beyond for me, and I appreciate every bit of feedback you give me. Amanda, thank you for getting to know my books so well and for knowing my voice when sometimes I get lost along the way. You're not only an amazing alpha reader, you're an incredible friend, and I'm thankful for you in so many ways.

Claire, Malissa, Valerie, and Azucena, thank you for taking the time to read this and give me your thoughts. Beta reading is so important to me and I love that I can count on you to push me to do better and to shape the book into what I want it to be.

To my ARC readers—thank you for your continued excitement for my books and for supporting each new release I have. I value you guys so much and am so lucky to have you on my team!

My family has always been by my side, supporting me and cheering me on from the very beginning. Thank you for constantly believing in me. I couldn't ask for a better support system than what I have with you guys. Best parents and sister ever!

As always, a big, giant thank you to my hubby Richard, who helps make my dreams a reality. I love you and can't wait to be able to retire you someday as we take trips around the world and live OUR dreams together.

My sweet girls. You're getting older and your love for reading still amazes me. I hope that fire always burns brightly inside you and that you continue to find joy in books, just like I do. Never settle for less than what you want. Work hard and keep pushing. You'll be amazed at what you're capable of, my loves.

Thank you again to everyone who has taken the time to read this story. If you'd love to leave your thoughts in a review, I would greatly appreciate it. Thank you!

# About the Author

Samantha lives in the southwest with her husband and two small children after abandoning her childhood dream of living in a cabin in Colorado when she found that she couldn't afford to live there and was deathly allergic to the woods. When she's not writing, she's usually spouting off sarcastic remarks while drinking wine out of a coffee mug to look like a functional adult while chasing down her toddlers. She enjoys spending time with her family, watching reruns of Friends, and the 24/7 flow of coffee that can be found in her veins. Be sure to follow her on social media for updates on what she's working on.

You can find her here:

Facebook: https://www.facebook.com/AuthorSamanthaBaca

Instagram: https://instagram.com/author_samantha_baca

Goodreads: http://www.goodreads.com/authorsamanthabaca

Facebook Reader Group:

https://www.facebook.com/groups/2945710968775398/

Webpage: https://authorsamanthabaca.wordpress.com

Newsletter: http://eepurl.com/g0NcSj